Noah's Ride

Noah's Ride

A COLLABORATIVE WESTERN NOVEL BY

ELMER KELTON

JUDY ALTER

CARLTON STOWERS

PHYLLIS ALLEN

JAMES REASONER

MARY ROGERS

MIKE COCHRAN

MIKE BLACKMAN

MARY DITTOE KELLY

JANE ROBERTS WOOD

JAMES WARD LEE

CAROLE NELSON DOUGLAS

JEFF GUINN

Texas Christian University Press / Fort Worth

Copyright © TCU Press 2006

Library of Congress Cataloging-in-Publication Data

Noah's Ride : a collaborative novel / edited by Judy Alter and Jeff Guinn.
    p. cm.
  ISBN-13: 978-0-87565-334-1 (trade paper : alk. paper)
  1. Slavery—Texas—Fiction. 2. Fugitive slaves—Fiction. 3. Texas—
Fiction. 4. Christian fiction. I. Alter, Judy, 1938- II. Guinn, Jeff.
  PS3600.A1N63 2006
  813'.6—dc22

                                             2006016230

Printed in Canada

TCU Press, P.O. Box 298300, Fort Worth, TX 76129
817.257.7822 <http://www.prs.tcu.edu>
To order books: 1.800.826.8911

Design: Shadetree Studio

For Jerry Flemmons,
who inspired and encouraged many of us
and who strongly supported
the first suggestion of
a Texas collaborative novel
several years ago

Chapter One

by Elmer Kelton

Noah heard the hounds baying behind him and knew they were catching up. He feared his heart was about to explode. Moaning in panic, struggling for breath, he plunged headlong through needle-sharp briars that blocked his path. They scratched his dark face and clutched at his ragged clothing, trying to hold him back. The river must not be far ahead. If he could reach that, perhaps he could throw the dogs off the scent. Otherwise, the slave catchers would soon have him. In his imagination he already felt the pain of the lash. He knew what it would be like, for he had been whipped before.

His knees quivered from fatigue. It took all his will to force one foot in front of the other. Only the sound of the bloodhounds gave him strength to keep struggling. Soon even that was not enough. His legs buckled, and he fell headlong, crying out in frustration and fear. He fought to regain his feet but could not. He moved forward on hands and knees.

He was quickly surrounded by half a dozen flop-eared hounds, baying to their masters that they had run their quarry down. Noah heard a man shout, "We got him."

He slowly raised his eyes. Within touching distance were the largest feet he had ever seen, encased in worn-out lace-up shoes slit on the sides to lessen the burn of bunions. He looked up a long pair of legs thick as tree trunks to a huge set of shoulders broad as a barn door, and finally to a stubbled black face and white-rimmed eyes devoid of expression.

In tones deep and strong, like the voice of doom, the huge man said, "Don't you move, or I'll bust your head."

He had fallen into the hands of Goliath, the dull-minded enforcer of old Massa Ellerbee's law. Goliath had been given that name for his size, his brute strength, his unyielding dominance over the slave quarters. He had been known to knock down a grown mule with his massive fist. No one was ever sure what he might do. For the most part he did as he pleased, for even the white overseer was a little afraid of him. Only old Massa had full control. He pulled Goliath's strings as if the giant were a puppet.

One of the white slave catchers ordered, "Fetch that black devil over here."

Goliath lifted Noah to his feet, but Noah could not stand. The giant picked him up and threw him over a heavy shoulder as if he were a sack of grain. "It don't look like he can walk no more," he said.

"Put him on this mule," the catcher commanded.

Goliath lifted Noah onto the mule's bare back. Its sharp spine cut like straddling a board fence. The catcher looped a rope around Noah's neck and said, "You better not fall off, or you'll strangle. If it was up to me I'd hang you anyway, but Old Man Ellerbee claims you're worth two thousand dollars."

Noah had run away before, increasing the severity of the punishment likely to be inflicted upon him. He had run this time after talking back to his owner, a crime sure to bring severe punishment. His running would make that punishment even worse. He could take comfort in one point: They would not kill him. He was too valuable a property. For something worse than running, however, they might.

The mule lagged, and Noah choked. The rope burned his neck. He could hear the white men talking among themselves, speculating how much reward Ellerbee would pay for a two-thousand-dollar nigger.

One said, "If he'd got to the Yankee forces, we'd never've got him back."

Noah had not even thought of trying to reach the Yankee troops. He had been lectured that they were to be feared like Old Lucifer, that they killed southerners without pity, whether white or black. Word from up the river was that they were invading the South with such ever-increasing strength that some folks were beginning to wonder if the Confederacy was losing the war. It was a prospect said to bring fear even to Massa Ellerbee, and Massa had always acted as if he was not afraid of anything.

The Yankees must be in league with the devil, Noah thought. He knew a lot about the devil. Ellerbee saw to it that all his slaves attended Sunday services, where a minister preached about the hellfire that awaited if they did not work hard and obey their masters. He painted a frightening picture. Noah had trembled through many a sermon.

In spite of the minister's dark message, Noah had sometimes allowed himself to question why there were slaves and masters. The only difference he could see between himself and most white people of his acquaintance was that his skin was black. True, the white folks seemed to know more. They could read newspapers and books. Slaves were forbidden to learn to read because, as the parson explained, it might give them false notions and lead them into mischief. On the other hand, Noah was physically stronger than almost any white man he had ever seen. He stood taller than most, had wider shoulders and more muscular arms than most. About the only stronger man on the plantation was Goliath. He was a head taller than Noah, and broader by far. The only thing weak about him was his mind. He would stick both hands in a bucket of coals if Massa told him to.

Besides the strength that allowed him to work like a mule, Goliath had proven his ability to sire male children who promised to grow up big and strong like himself. Ellerbee used him to service female slaves in hope of raising a crop of hard workers. When he could spare him, he leased him out to neighboring slave owners in the same manner that he sold the services of his black stallion for other people's mares.

Noah had heard Massa say that Goliath was worth his weight in Yankee gold.

Ellerbee came down from the big house as the catchers returned with Noah. His eyes were fierce, his mouth a broad grim line between a heavy gray mustache and trimmed chin whiskers. "Tie him to that gate post yonder," he ordered. "Goliath, fetch my whip."

The catchers did as they were told, first stripping Noah's torn shirt from him, then tying his hands to the post so tightly that the rope cut into his wrists. One said, "From the looks of the scars on his back, he's run away before. He'll do it again. If I was you, Mr. Ellerbee, I'd sell him down the river for whatever I could get. Palm him off on somebody else like you'd get rid of a blind horse."

"I would, but he's a hard worker when he behaves himself. And I'll teach him to behave himself if I have to kill him first. Goliath, hurry up with that blacksnake."

Goliath's big shadow fell across Noah as he uncoiled the whip. "You goin' to do it, Massa?"

"No, you do it. Be careful you don't let it curl around his face. He wouldn't be of much use to me blind,"

Noah heard the whip sing before it burned white-hot across his back. He heard a scream and knew it came from his own throat. He cringed, dreading the next strike. It came with more ferocity than the first. He tried at first to count the lashings, but in his agony he lost track. His crying faded to a weak whimper.

He heard Massa say, "That's enough. A dead nigger ain't worth the shovel it takes to bury him with." Massa moved up close enough that Noah could smell whiskey on his breath. Ellerbee said, "Now listen to me, boy. You'd better learn to be good, or I'll sell you to somebody mean."

Goliath untied the rope that bound Noah's wrists. Noah slid slowly down the post to the ground. He heard Massa say, "Uncle Jonah, take care of him. I want him back in the field in a couple of days."

Though a reddish haze Noah felt a pair of gentle hands trying to lift him up. The old man had been a good field hand in his time, but age had taken his strength. "Goliath," he said, "come help me get him to my cabin."

Goliath easily hoisted Noah up over one shoulder. The stretching brought a rush of searing pain, and Noah groaned.

Goliath showed no sympathy. "You brung it on yourself." He asked Uncle Jonah, "Where's your granddaughter at?"

"Nelly's out in the field workin', like she's supposed to be."

"I been watchin' her. That gal's gettin' to be right good-lookin'."

"She ain't for you, Goliath. She's too young yet." The old man's voice carried a sense of anxiety.

"Some flowers bloom early."

Noah had been watching Nelly too. She wasn't much bigger than Ellerbee's watchfob, but she was already making the field hands straighten up from their work and take notice. At the moment, however, he hurt too much to let his mind dwell on Nelly or anything else except the fire that blazed all across his back.

Goliath carried him into a small log cabin that leaned a little with age.

Uncle Jonah said, "Lay him down on my cot." His voice sharpened. "Not on his back, on his stomach."

Goliath complied, then stepped aside. He said, "Mind what Massa told you. He wants him workin' in a day or two. Them as don't work don't eat."

"He can't do much, the shape he's in."

"Maybe he'll remember next time he takes a notion to run off."

When Goliath was gone, Uncle Jonah said, "I ain't got nothin' to treat you with except some hog lard. Maybe it'll ease the burnin' a little."

First he washed the blood away with a wet cloth, which started the fire all over again. He waited for Noah's back to dry, then applied handfuls of lard, spreading it gently across the whip cuts. "Bacon grease would heal you faster maybe, but the salt in it would eat you alive."

Noah dug his fingers into Jonah's frazzled old blanket and tried to keep from crying out. He half wished the catchers had shot him. He wouldn't be hurting so much now. He slowly lapsed into a half sleep, or perhaps it was semi-consciousness. He dreamed of being bigger and stronger than Goliath and lashing him with Massa's whip. He took a couple of licks at Massa too and felt pleasure in the wickedness of a fantasy he knew would never come true.

* * *

He became aware that the cabin was darkening. He could hear the mutter of conversation among field hands coming home to supper in the several cabins along slave row. He made out a slender figure, pausing in the cabin door. A girl's voice said, "I heard what happened to Noah, Granpaw. You got him here?"

"What's left of him. I think he's awake if you want to talk to him."

Nelly knelt beside the cot. Hesitantly she reached out a tiny hand as if to touch his wounds, then drew it back. She placed it on his arm instead. "You goin' to be all right, ain't you, Noah?"

Noah warmed a little at her presence. "Ain't no whip fixin' to kill me. I'll get away the next time."

She looked around as if afraid some outsider might be listening. "You'd try again? They liable to kill you."

"Not if I can get a far piece across the river."

"I wish you'd take me with you. I'd give anything to get away from here. I hate the way that old Goliath keeps lookin' at me. I know what he's thinkin'."

Noah wished he could give her a promise, but he knew it would be futile. It would be hard enough to escape by himself. Getting away with this girl on his hands would be even harder. She could run like a deer for a short distance, but she would not have the stamina for a long chase.

Uncle Jonah was at his small table, slicing a chunk of hog fat with a butcher knife. He said, "I'd like to use this on Goliath. At least a part of him."

She said, "Don't talk thataway, Granpaw. Somebody might hear you."

"Ain't nobody goin' to tell."

She said, "Maybe we won't have to go noplace. They're sayin' the Yankees ain't far up the river, and they're comin' this way. One of these days I expect Massa will be leavin' here, runnin' like a scalded dog."

It hurt Noah to talk, but he said, "What good'll them Yankees do us? Folks say they kill everybody they come across."

"That's white folks talkin'. The Yankees are comin' to set us free."

Such a notion went against all of Noah's experience. The Yankees were white. He figured that if they came, they would just be a different set of owners. He would be expected to answer to a new master instead of Ellerbee, but a master just the same.

"I don't need nobody to set me free. All I need is a good runnin' start."

Uncle Jonah suggested, "He needs some more lard rubbed onto his back. Why don't you do it, Nelly?"

Under other circumstances Noah would have enjoyed the gentle touch of her hands, but now it caused him pain. The lard was cool and soothing, once she quit rubbing it in. She said, "I'll come back and do it again in the mornin' before I leave for the field."

Nelly left, headed for a cabin she shared with two older women. Though she was accepted as Jonah's granddaughter, she was not blood kin. His own children sold off, the old man had simply taken a protective interest in her when she was six years old. Her mother had been sold to a new owner in some faraway place, but the new Massa couldn't be bothered with a girl too young to do much work.

Noah tried to arise. Old Jonah motioned for him to stay put. "I'll sleep on a pallet. You'd best lay still as you can and let them cuts heal."

"Before I leave here I'd like to hit Goliath up side the head with a singletree."

"Goliath could bust you into little bitty pieces and not break a sweat. Better you go way around him from now on, like you'd go way around a skunk."

"He smells might near as bad."

"To Massa, he smells like money."

Noah lay around the cabin the next day, the cuts bringing agony. Nelly came to see him after quitting time. "How you feelin' now, Noah?"

"I feel like gettin' away from this place."

"Where you think you'd go?"

"Somewhere there ain't no masters, and no slaves."

"Old preacher says there ain't no such place, not till we get to Heaven. Then he says everything'll be different. But we got to work hard and do like we're told, or we'll go to the other place and burn for all eternity. How long do you reckon eternity is?"

"A good while, I expect. Seems like I been on this place for that long."

"You reckon runaways ever get to heaven?"

"I don't know, but hell can't be much worse than what we got here."

He made his way to the field the next day, but he found he could do little. He felt the overseer's gaze from time to time and tried to give the appearance of working. The overseer came to him eventually and said, "Noah, I got a jug of cool water yonder in the shade of that tree. Why don't you go over there and set down? Watch the jug for me, and move it if the sun starts to get on it. Ain't nothin' I hate worse than to drink warm water."

Noah was not used to kindness from an overseer. "Yes, sir. I'll keep it in the shade."

He did not have to be told not to drink from the jug. White folks would consider that contamination.

He protected the overseer's water the rest of that day and all of the next.

Goliath came around once and studied him with suspicion. "Old Massa ain't goin' to take it kindly, he sees you settin'."

"I'm doin' what the overseer told me to."

Nelly came around to share the shade with Noah while nobody was looking. She sat beside him and said, "You look like you feel better."

"Them places are itchin' somethin' awful. Reckon that means they're startin' to heal."

"When you figurin' on lightin' out?"

"Not till the healin's done and I got all my strength back. I don't aim for them to catch me next time."

"I sure wish I could go."

"I wish you could, too, but I'm afraid you'd play out too quick. I couldn't carry you and outrun them dogs."

A deep, gruff voice startled both of them. Goliath had come up from behind. "Gal, what you doin' here gossupin' when you're supposed to be out yonder a-workin'?"

Frightened, Nelly leaped to her feet and ran off into the field. Goliath stared after her with wishing eyes. "Looks to me like she's about ready."

Noah was afraid he knew, but he asked anyway. "Ready for what?"

"For me. I see Massa over at the far edge of the field. I believe I'll go ask him."

Noah's own pain was forgotten a while. He felt fear for Nelly but did not know anything he could do to help her.

At quitting time he trudged back from the field with the other hands. Nelly walked beside him, matching his pace. He wanted to put his arm around her and protect her, but he was helpless to do anything meaningful. He could only say, "You better stay as far away from Goliath as you can."

"You think he's mad at me because he caught me restin' in the shade?"

"I'm afraid that ain't what he's got on his mind."

Nelly nodded gravely. Her voice held a tremor. "He's a big, fearsome man."

"And you're a tiny little girl." An ugly image bullied its way into his imagination. He tried without success to banish it. "Maybe you ought to run off into the woods and hide tonight."

"I can't hide every night. Sooner or later . . ."

"Then go to Aunt Suse. She's about the only one that can make Goliath bow his head. She won't let him touch you." Aunt Suse was one of the oldest women on the plantation. Even Ellerbee spoke to her with respect. The preacher had said more than once that she had the tongue of an adder, whatever an adder was.

Jonah was slicing sidemeat with a butcher knife when Noah walked in. He laid the knife down and said, "Let me look at your back."

Noah lifted his shirt. Jonah frowned. "It ain't pretty, but maybe you've seen the worst. I'll have us some supper fixed directly."

"I ain't done enough work to get hungry."

"You'll eat anyway. You need your strength."

They were in the midst of supper when Noah heard an anguished scream. He looked at Jonah and saw fear leap into the old man's eyes. Jonah said, "That sounds like Nelly." He tried to rise up from behind the table but was slowed by his arthritic legs.

Noah beat him to the door. Nelly rushed in, crying hysterically. "It's Goliath. He's after me."

Noah pushed her toward Jonah and braced himself in the doorway. He saw the huge form looming in the dusk, moving toward him.

Goliath's voice boomed. "Git out of my way."

Noah stood his ground. "You ain't gettin' her."

"Massa says she's old enough to bear." He extended a muscular arm and pushed against Noah's shoulder. "Move, I said."

"And I said you ain't gettin' her. Go on, Goliath. She ain't ready yet."

Goliath gave him a harder shove. Noah stumbled backward but caught his footing and grabbed Goliath's arms. They were hard as iron. "No, Goliath. There's other women."

Goliath broke free of him and brought a ham-sized fist up against the side of Noah's head. Noah felt as if his brain had exploded. He went to his knees, grabbing at the edge of the table in an effort to break his fall. He saw Jonah rush at Goliath. The old man shouted, "You can't have her."

Goliath flung him across the little room as if he were a rag doll.

Nelly screamed as Goliath grabbed her thin arm. "Come on. You fixin' to go with me."

Noah reached out to grab at Goliath. The big man struck him in the face, knocking him back against the table. Noah tasted blood and knew his lip was torn. Nelly screamed again. "Noah!"

Bracing himself against the table, Noah felt a sting as the butcher knife cut into his fingers. He flinched, then with a bleeding hand picked up the knife by its handle. Without taking time to consider, he threw himself in front of Goliath again and plunged the blade between the man's ribs.

Goliath's eyes bulged in confusion and pain, meeting Noah's in disbelief. He staggered. Nelly broke away from him and ran to Jonah. The old man took her in his arms and watched in horror as Goliath lurched against the doorjamb, then out into the deepening dusk.

Noah followed, trying to comprehend what had happened.

Goliath stopped, looking back accusingly toward Noah. His voice seemed to rattle. "Massa told me to." He wavered, and went down like a felled oak.

Noah could only stare at him, not quite believing what he had done. He was conscious of other people gathering, drawn by Nelly's screams and the sound of the fight in Jonah's cabin. One man drummed up courage enough to lean down and touch Goliath's body, then drew back quickly as if a snake had bitten him. The people began to move away from Noah, their faces contorted in shock and fear.

Jonah nervously made his way to Noah's side. Nelly stopped in the doorway, still sobbing hysterically. Jonah acted as if he were going to touch Goliath, to see if he was really dead, but he backed away. An awful anguish was in his eyes. "You know what you've done, Noah?"

Noah had difficulty in finding voice. "Looks like I've killed Goliath."

"You've killed yourself, too, less'n you get away from here fast. It don't matter now how much you're worth to Massa. They'll hang you up by the neck, and then they'll burn you like they'd roast a hog."

"I ain't got all my strength back. I can't run fast enough that they can't catch me."

Jonah trembled. "That brown saddle mule Ezra's been ridin' . . . it's out yonder in the pen. I've seen Ezra run it pretty fast."

Noah had ridden a mule from time to time. He was not an expert rider, but he could stay on. "Ezra might not like it."

"You ain't got time to worry about what Ezra might like. You got to git, and git now!"

Aunt Suse had taken charge of Nelly, enveloping her in heavy arms and speaking softly to her as if she were a small child. Her gaze lifted to Noah. "You better do like Jonah says, and git."

His mouth dry and his heart racing, Noah trotted to the pen where the work mules had been turned for the night. Ezra's stood at a hay rack, filling its belly. Noah grabbed a bridle from the shed and put his arms around the mule's neck until he had the bit in its mouth and the bridle over its head. He turned toward the saddle rack.

Jonah stood at the gate, holding it open wide enough for Noah to lead the mule outside. He said, "Aunt Suse is sackin' you up some pork and some cornbread. You better ride all night."

"I don't know where to go."

"To the river, and way past on the other side. Maybe you'll run onto some Yankee soldiers."

"I'm afraid of them."

"You'd better be a lot more afraid of what'll be doggin' your trail. Maybe the Yankees will protect you. At least they won't burn you alive."

Aunt Suse brought a sack of food as Jonah had promised.

Noah asked her, "What about Nelly?"

She said urgently, "Don't you be frettin' about Nelly. I'll see after her. You make sure you don't let Massa's men catch you. Now go before the ruckus brings the overseer down here."

Against his will, Noah took a quick last look at the still body of Goliath and at the row of cabins he was leaving. This had been the only home he had known most of his life. He had never known who his father was, somebody like Goliath perhaps. He remembered his mother clearly, even though he was still a young boy when he was sold away from her. Massa Ellerbee felt he had gotten a bargain on a young buck who looked to grow into a strong hand.

He had no way to know how long it might be before the white folks discovered that Goliath was dead. Nobody on slave row was likely to volunteer that information for fear of being linked to the killing. Nobody would admit at first to having seen anything, though some were certain to spill the whole story once they felt the threat of a whip.

He knew from whispered tales that an occasional runaway had managed to make it to freedom somewhere to the north. He had no idea how far that might be, or how many slave catchers he might encounter on the way. But he knew the river lay to the west. He had almost made it that far the last time, until exhaustion brought him down. He had been afoot then. Now at least he had a mule.

He put the mule into a run but realized soon that the animal could not hold that pace for long. It had put in a day's work already. He tugged on the reins and brought it down to a rough trot. He felt that his innards were jarring loose, but he had to accept it. What awaited him back there was infinitely worse.

He pushed through the night, finding a wagon road and following it, hoping his tracks would be lost among the many already there. The trail was crooked, passing around groves of trees, skirting the edge of fields, leading past dark houses. It seemed that at every house he aroused a pack of barking dogs. He held his breath, fearing someone would come out to investigate.

Once, so close that it startled him, he heard someone shout, "Hey, you dogs, hush up before I shoot the lot of you." Noah feared the man would see him in the moonlight. He brought the mule to a stop and tried to stand still as a statue until he felt that the man had gone back into the house. He put the mule into a slow walk, hoping to make the least possible amount of noise until he was well past sight.

At least these were just plain mongrel dogs, not bloodhounds.

Daylight brought him little comfort. He had never been this far from the plantation, at least within his memory. He had no idea where he was. The rising sun was at his back, so he knew he was still traveling in a westerly direction. The river must lie somewhere ahead.

An hour after sunup, he ran suddenly into three white men on horseback. They reined up and confronted him. One with a gray-streaked black beard eased close and demanded, "I don't know you, boy. Where you goin'?"

Noah's heart skipped. He swallowed hard and mustered courage, grabbing at an excuse. Where it came from, he would never know. "Massa sent me to deliver this mule. Sold him to a man over by the river."

"You got anything to prove that? A note or somethin'?" The voice sounded threatening, though that could have been Noah's imagination.

Noah said, "No, sir. He just told me that I was to take this mule to Mr. Johnson." He pulled the name out of the air. "Mr. Will Johnson."

"Seems odd that he'd send you all by yourself, with nothin' to show that what you say is the gospel. Who do you belong to?"

Noah saw no reason to lie about that. News of the killing could not have gotten this far. "Massa Ellerbee."

One of the other men spoke up. "I know Old Man Ellerbee. He's a penny-pinchin' old skinflint who's got a farm over east." He turned his attention to Noah. "You look pretty husky, boy. I've heard Ellerbee has got a big nigger by the name of Goliath that he puts out to stud. Is that your name?"

Noah nodded and tried to keep his voice steady. "Yes, sir. That's what they call me. Goliath."

"You ain't as big as the stories they tell about you, but I guess nobody ever is." He glanced at the older man. "I hear Ellerbee trusts him to go by himself to wherever he's told. I reckon I'd be glad to take orders too if I had the job he's got." He grinned wickedly. "Get along on your way, boy, and count your blessin's."

"Yes, sir. Thank you, sir."

Noah rode on, fighting down a strong temptation to look back and see if they were following. Fright had caused his stomach to turn over and threatened to make him throw up.

He moved the mule into a faster trot, putting distance between him and the three men. They would have taken him in hand without hesitation if they had not believed his story. He would not likely have lived to see the sun go down.

It struck him as ironic that he had killed Goliath, yet Goliath had indirectly saved his life.

* * *

Within minutes of learning that Noah had fled, Massa Ellerbee had stomped into his study and sent for the slave catcher Quint. Within an hour the man knocked at the door and then walked in.

Ellerbee looked at the one-eyed man for a moment. Then he said, "That nigger Noah that killed Goliath has run away. I want you to find him. Here's a letter of introduction and a hundred dollars. There's another hundred when you get back. Take one or two of your boys if you like."

Quint lived in a filthy shambles of a house with his four sons, each one born of a different slave. No white woman would have the slave catcher with the long, greasy hair and milky eye. Rumor had it that he drowned any baby he fathered that was born with kinky hair.

"I'll find him," Quint muttered. "You gonna' use the dogs here? I'll head for the river, 'cause I betcha that's where that nigger's goin'. Thinks he can get across 'fore I find him." He pounded his open palm with his fist in anger, as though he were crushing Noah.

"He killed the best breeding buck in these parts. It was like having a three-bale-an-acre-cotton crop every year. A real money-maker," said Ellerbee. "And Quint, don't bring him back here. Kill him. I want that green-eyed nigger dead. Always knew there was something wrong with a green-eyed nigger."

Quint's good eye seemed to light up at this instruction.

Chapter Two

by Judy Alter

Terror made cold sweat run down Noah's back as he rode, pushing the mule as fast as he dared until he got well away. Various unpleasant scenes flashed into his mind—another whipping, more severe but still survivable, or a lynching, or even a burning. When his mind took a turn like that, he focused on the river. It had become a symbol of safety, though he had no idea what was on the other side. He thought it had to be better than Mississippi, and maybe, as Jonah said, he'd find Yankee troops who would protect him. Then again, maybe not. But the one thing he knew for sure: Dogs couldn't track him across water.

Noah had no regrets about leaving Massa Ellerbee's place, even though it was the only home he'd ever known. Oh, he'd miss Jonah and Aunt Suse. They'd been good to him. And there was Nelly—the thought of her gave him a moment's hesitation. He wouldn't turn back, not ever, but he knew he'd miss Nelly. He remembered the way she'd gently touched the welts on his back. And he shuddered when he thought of how close she'd come to being raped by Goliath. That thought made Noah want to go back and send Massa Ellerbee to join Goliath, just for having given the giant permission. He could still hear Goliath's words, "Massa told me to." Noah knew someday soon Massa would "tell" one of his other slaves, and he knew he'd never see Nelly again. He pushed the thought out of his mind.

The mule had set a slow but steady pace, and every step it took jarred the soreness in Noah's back. He kept to the road but moved into the brush when he heard hoof beats, even in the distance. Sometimes he'd find a small creek where the mule could drink, and as the sun rose and the April day began to heat up, Noah began to thirst himself. He was always careful to drink before the mule, though he knew it probably was a foolish caution. By late afternoon the pork and cornbread Aunt Suse had sacked up for him were gone, and he felt the welts on his back as though they were all fresh. The mule had begun to slow down, and every once in a while it faltered. Noah wondered how long and how far he could go before it gave out—or he did.

They both gave out about the same time, just as it was turning dark. Noah held on long enough to get the mule off the road. Then he literally slid off, landing in a ditch. Just before he fell, Noah thought he saw a huge white house, with all the windows brightly lit, and thought perhaps he had died and that was one of the golden mansions in Heaven the preacher used to talk about. He slept as though he were indeed dead, waking only once in the night after a terrible nightmare in which Goliath had come after him with that butcher knife, and he had taken shelter in that huge white house. Noah woke surprised that he was alive, and then he propped himself up on one elbow and looked around vaguely for the mule. The effort was too much, and he fell back into the ditch again.

Hattie Kendrick first thought she saw a pile of rags in the ditch. Someone would be in big trouble if cotton bags or something else valuable had been thrown in that ditch! Then the rags stirred, and slowly a dark head emerged.

"What're you doing in the ditch, boy?" she demanded, hands on her hips.

Noah looked up at what he thought was an angel of some kind. Once again, he thought he had died and gone to Heaven, where that white mansion was, though he never imagined that angels looked quite like this girl. She was his age, maybe just a tad younger, clearly a slave but lighter-skinned than any slave Noah had ever seen—and better dressed. She wore a muslin dress under a starched white apron and had a white cap edged in lace on her head. It let just a few curls escape around her face, and her hair was coarse but not kinky and coal black like his. Noah had no idea what to make of her and just stared.

"I said, what you doing in the ditch?"

"I fell off my mule," he said weakly.

"Fell off your mule?" She started to laugh and then stopped short. She had noticed a mule out beyond the henhouse when she went to fetch eggs for Massa's breakfast. "So that's your mule I saw. Where you going with it, if you get it back?"

"You saw my mule? It's alive?"

She nodded. "It's alive. Looks like it needs some care though. Where you going?"

"The river," he said. "I got to cross the river."

"How you plan to get across it?"

Noah wondered why he felt foolish as he answered, "Swim."

Now she really did laugh, the sound bursting from someplace deep inside. "Swim," she gasped. "You got any idea how wide that river is?"

He shook his head miserably.

"You ain't swimming," she said.

Noah struggled to his feet and looked down at his clothes. His shirt was torn and dirty, and his pants were caked with mud from his night in the ditch. And he was suddenly aware that he was powerful hungry.

Hattie drew in a deep breath. "You're a runaway, aren't you?" She stared straight at Noah, took in the strength of his body, the defeat in his posture, and the greenest eyes she'd ever seen in her life. For a moment, she was startled. How could a slave who looked to be straight from Africa have green eyes?

Noah had never gambled in his life, not even when the slaves pitched horseshoes around a fire at night, but he looked her in the eye and gambled. "Yes, ma'am."

"You done something bad?" Her tone was demanding again.

"I guess. I killed a man."

"White man or slave?"

"Slave."

"He deserve killing?"

Noah nodded his head. No need to tell her the whole ugly story.

"Who you running from?"

"Massa Ellerbee." He nodded his head, as though showing her the location of the Ellerbee place.

She raised her hands in despair. "Oh, Lord, I heard of him. Mean. Works his slaves like oxen and whips them."

Noah thought maybe he should show her his back but decided against it.

"Let me think," she said, commanding him to silence with her tone. Then, after a minute, "We got to get you clean clothes, and you're probably hungry." When he nodded, she said, "I thought so." She looked at the basket in her hand. "I got to pick some cress down by the creek for Miz' Kendrick's lunch, and then I can take you to the slave quarters and fix you up. Go hide in that brush till I come get you."

Noah's eyes widened. "You ain't a slave!" In truth, he couldn't figure out what she was or how she fit in the scheme of things. She talked better than any colored girl he'd ever known. And there was her dress . . . and her lighter skin.

Hattie gazed across the road where she could see the field hands checking the tiny cotton plants that had been in the ground a month now, looking for bolls and thinning out any bold weeds. She looked down at her own hands—almost white and without calluses—and was grateful again that she had had a white father. She had often looked wonderingly at Massa Kendrick. After all, he'd given her his last name. "I'm a house servant," she said softly, "but I'm not free." Then her tone became brisk again. "Go on, get in that brush before the overseer sees you." She inclined her head toward the field where the slaves worked.

It seemed forever to Noah before she returned, but it was probably less than an hour. She stood in the road and called softly, "Stay in the bushes but follow where I go." And so, him in the bushes and her on the lane that ran around Cedar Grove plantation, they moved toward the slave cabins. When she motioned him out, he said, "I don't even know your name."

"I'm Hattie Kendrick. Who are you?"

"Noah."

"Your last name Ellerbee?"

He looked down at his feet. "I don't have no name but Noah," he said.

He found himself hustled into a cabin, where an old woman fed him stewed chicken, possibly the best he'd ever had, and a young woman, too pregnant to be in the fields, brought him a clean shirt and pants. "My husband's," she explained, and when he promised to get them back to her, she said, "I can make more. Massa's generous."

Noah had a hard time putting the idea of "Massa" and the word "generous" together. This massa must be really different from Massa Ellerbee.

It occurred to him maybe he should just stay here and work in the fields with the people Hattie had pointed out. The idea of seeing Hattie frequently didn't seem all bad, and neither did life at Cedar Grove. But then he remembered the fate that waited him if Massa Ellerbee found him, as he surely would, and he said anxiously, "I got to be goin'. Thanks to all of you."

He rose but the young woman pushed him down. "Hattie says you're to wait here for her. She'll get someone to take you to Vicksburg."

"Vicksburg?" he echoed incredulously.

"That's where the river is," Hattie said as she came into the cabin. "George has got to take a load of china and things to Vicksburg. Miz' is shipping the whole house, piece by piece, to relatives for safekeeping. She thinks the Yankees will be here soon."

"Yankees? Is that good or bad?" By now, Noah was confused about a lot of things.

"Good for us," Hattie said dryly. "Not so good for plantation owners. George can put you under a tarp and take you to Vicksburg. He'll help you find a way to get across the river. Meantime, stay inside today and have a good sleep tonight. Lord knows when you'll get a good night's sleep again."

Noah did as he was told and spent the day hidden in the old woman's cabin—he had learned her name was Belle and everyone called her Auntibelle, as though it were all one word. Noah spent much of the day trying to avoid the image of Goliath lying dead that kept popping up in his mind. And then he'd remember the times Goliath had beaten him. Sometimes his mind wandered back to the plantation in Alabama, where he'd lived with his mother and his sister, Lovie. He remembered how Lovie clung to Mama the day they took him away in chains, him not more than eleven or twelve. And he remembered how he'd told Lovie not to worry—he'd find her and take care of her someday. Where, he wondered, is Lovie now?

After a supper of more stewed chicken, when it was good dark, Hattie appeared. "I just got Miz' settled for the night, but I don't dare stay long. She's liable to call for me any old time. I told her I was coming down to check on Auntibelle, who's not been feeling too good."

"I feels fine," Auntibelle protested.

Hattie turned to Noah. "Where you going when you get across the river? Louisiana's got slaves too, you know."

So that was what's across the river. Noah tried to digest the information. "I guess I'll just keep goin'. Maybe get to Texas sometime. I heard tell once that it was a pretty free place."

Hattie shook her head. "I don't know if they got slaves or not. But it's worth a try." She looked at him. "You take care of yourself, Noah. You're a good person. And if anyone from Massa Ellerbee's comes here, nobody's ever seen you."

Noah returned her direct look. "I thank you, Hattie, for all you done. I'm sorry to say goodbye to you." He thought about taking her hand and then decided better of it.

She shrugged and smiled. "You're a good person, Noah." Then, lightly, she kissed him on the cheek and disappeared into the night.

Auntibelle shook him awake before dawn. She gave him a sack of cornbread with cracklin's in it and wished him Godspeed.

He found himself in a wagon, crouched on the bed, having to curl up between the carefully wrapped furniture that filled most of the wagon bed. George had thrown a tarp over him, and Noah imagined that from outside the wagon he looked like another footstool or something stuffed in between the armoire and chairs.

For many miles, there was silence from the mysterious George, such silence that Noah began to think wild thoughts, like maybe this was all a hoax, and George was really taking him back to Massa Ellerbee to be roasted alive. His muscles cramped from the position, and he longed to at least throw back the tarp enough to see his driver. But he dared not move, and besides, there was no space around him.

Sometimes, lying there, he thought about Hattie. She was still a puzzle to him —her light skin, her manners. And then he thought about Nelly and how hard her life had been. He just didn't understand how two women could be slaves and treated so different.

Finally, George spoke, softly. "Lie special still now, boy. Here comes horsemen."

The tarp had muffled the sound, but too soon Noah too heard the hooves pounding on the road.

"You there," called a rough, white voice. "You seen a slave, about six foot tall, muscular? With green eyes? Probably pretty tired by now."

Noah held his breath when he recognized the voice of Quint, the slave catcher. He'd seen Quint's cruelty to other slaves, and the idea that the man with the funny eye was on his trail sent a whole new shock of terror through him.

"No, sir, I ain't seen nobody." George had brought the wagon to a stop, and Noah could hear the horses circling it.

"What you got in there, boy?"

"Things Miz' Kendrick's sending over to Louisiana. She's 'fraid the Yankees are comin'. Doesn't want 'em to get her good stuff, so she's shipping it to her sister."

Another voice laughed heartily. Noah suspected it was one of Quint's bastard sons. "You tell that Miz' she's got nothing to worry about. Our boys will whip 'em. Ain't we been standing 'em off at Vicksburg for months now?"

"Yessir, we sure have," George replied.

"You better hope we keep 'em away," said yet another voice. "They'll kill every nigger they get their hands on." Then he went on, "I know Kendrick. He's a straight shooter, and I know you ain't hidin' no slave."

He's got some of his sons with him, thought Noah, calculating on how much more perilous that made his situation.

"Yessir," George repeated again.

"You keep an eye out for him, though," Quint said. "His name's Noah. Ellerbee's beatin' the bushes back at the plantation, but I think that buck may be going to Vicksburg. Somebody saw him riding a mule right down the road. Lied to them, he did, about delivering that mule for Ellerbee."

"Yessir," George said carefully. "I'll keep an eye out."

"Good. One way or another, I'm gonna kill me a nigger . . . slow."

Then Noah heard horses racing away. He did not move a muscle. George jogged the mules back into motion, and the wagon moved slowly—painfully slowly, Noah thought—down the rough road.

"I guess you can come on out now. Anybody asks, I can explain you as a new slave, going to help me load this stuff onto the ship in Vicksburg."

Noah turned and stretched as much as room allowed, the ropey, torn muscles in his back protesting the movement. Then, slowly, he turned so that he could see George. "I ain't comin' up there on that seat. I know what Quint would do to me if'n he catches me."

"You got to come out 'fore we get to Vicksburg," George said. "Can't have you crawlin' out of the wagon bed in the midst of town. Here." He handed him a battered straw hat. "Put this on. I'll just tell anybody you're a new slave, helping me deliver goods."

"But Quint . . . what if he comes back?"

George spat over the side of the wagon. "He long gone to Vicksburg. They ain't comin' back till they sure you ain't there." He reached down on the floor of the wagon and handed Noah a floppy, worn straw hat. "Here, put this on. You'll look different."

"But I will be in Vicksburg!" Noah's voice almost rose in a wail.

"They won't never find you, not with all them people. Don't worry. I got it all figured."

Noah looked at George. He was older, gray around the edges of his hair and on his face, but Noah couldn't tell how old. George kept his attention on the mules pulling the wagon, while Noah nervously watched the road behind them and in front.

"You'll make yourself dizzy," George said, "turning to and fro like that." Then he began to talk, slowly, almost as if to himself. "Yankees all around Vicksburg," he said. "Been there since before Christmas. Been trying to take the town, but so far, they ain't had no luck. Our soldiers done beat them back when they tried to come by the river and across land by the railroad route. Then they tried to approach from the north, through the swamps and bayous. Now they've gone south. That's why Miz' Kendrick figures it's time to send things upriver some to Louisiana. Soldiers are all south of Vicksburg—or directly across the river. Southern boys are good fighters, but Quint man is wrong. The Yankees be here soon enough."

Noah wondered how a slave knew so much about the movement of the Yankees. But he ventured a different question. "You want the Yankees to come?"

George shrugged. "I ain't got it bad where I am. What I gonna do different if they free us?"

"But . . . ." Noah started but was interrupted.

"I know. There's lots of niggers that are treated awful, and they ought to be free. Don't know though how they'll feed themselves. Still it ain't for me to decide. Good Lord knows what he's doing."

Noah fervently hoped he was right about that.

"Hear you want to cross the river, son."

Noah nodded. He thought once he had George talking, he best let him talk on.

"There's colored soldiers fighting for the Union across the river," he said. "You might see if you can't join up with them."

Colored soldiers! Another idea that Noah could barely grasp. Who would give a colored man a rifle? And yet, if they were soldiers . . .

George sensed his confusion. "I hear tell there's whole companies, or whatever you call them, that are colored. And they're right across the river. I'll help you get across that river, and then you're on your own."

Noah nodded, the knot of fear in his stomach softening to a growing sense of excitement—colored soldiers! The idea that he could be a soldier fascinated him. He remembered the hymn they sang in those services Massa Ellerbee made them attend: "Onward Christian Soldiers, marching as to war." Surely that wasn't what Massa intended—and maybe not what the Lord intended—but he could see himself fighting alongside Union troops to free the slaves.

So much had the soldier idea captivated his mind that he didn't notice the change in the land around them. He looked up to see the trees were thicker and the land more rolling. They went up a long hill and suddenly, at the top, he looked down on more houses clustered together than he had ever imagined in one place. And beyond that he could see the river. Hattie was sure right—he could never swim that. Why, it stretched farther across than some of Massa Ellerbee's fields. Sometimes planting cotton, he could barely drag himself across one of those fields. He, who'd learned to swim in that small creek on the Massa's property, could never swim that far.

But the houses were all close together. "Who lives there?" he asked George.

He shrugged. "Folks with money. Some with plantations keep houses in town. And there's merchants, and shipping men, and . . . well, houses where white men go to meet women."

George was puzzled. "What about colored men?"

"I s'pose they got some of those too. Never looked. I got me a woman. And I don't think slaves can go to those places."

Noah shook his head in wonderment. "I can't imagine wantin' to live on top of each other like that. I had all Massa Ellerbee's money, I'd live like he does, far away from other folks."

George just gave him a tolerant smile.

When they got down the hill and into the town, Noah saw that many of the buildings sat on bluffs, well above the river. He'd heard about rivers flooding—the creeks around Massa Ellerbee's overran their banks in the spring—and he supposed this huge river could flood in a mighty way. Living on the bluff was probably a good idea.

To Noah, used to the sparse population at Massa Ellerbee's place, the sight of people everywhere was . . . well, he didn't know what to say it was. The streets were rutted and rough, and he saw finely dressed women—better than Miz' Ellerbee ever dressed—picking their way across the ruts, usually but not always on the arm of some well-dressed gentleman. And everywhere he looked, he saw soldiers wearing that gray uniform. They frightened him, but he tried to hide his fright from George. Mostly he watched for Quint. He knew that if the overseer found him, George, too, was a dead man. Noah supposed George realized that, and he was grateful to the man for the risk he was taking.

Noah tried to sit still, but he fidgeted, and his eyes darted all around him. He longed for dark but that looked to be hours away.

George pulled up in front of a shanty built near the water's edge, under the bluffs. It was one of a string of flimsy shacks that reminded Noah of the slave quarters back home. Glad to be off the streets of Vicksburg, he followed George inside.

An older woman was busy stirring a pot of something that smelled so good Noah felt the muscles in his stomach tighten in anticipation. Without ever looking up at George, she said, "I figured you be coming this way soon. Miz' Kendrick fixing to send off more stuff?"

"She is," George said. Noah noticed that he dropped the "sir" and "ma'am" and "thank you" that he used when talking to whites. "I'm shippin' something too."

She turned now and saw Noah. "Where you shippin' him?"

"'Cross the river. What you heard about the Yankees?"

"Word is they're mostly still south of here, but southern boys are preparing to fight in either direction. And the Yankees are right across the river. You can almos' look out in the daytime and see them."

George harrumphed but only said, "You gonna feed us and let us sleep?"

"Of course."

George turned to Noah. "This here's Martha. Massa Kendrick freed her some fifteen years back. She's my woman, and she's why he trusts me to come to Vicksburg."

"Why he trust you to come back?" Noah asked.

"Hattie's Martha's daughter."

Noah nodded. He knew Hattie wasn't George's flesh, but in spirit she was his child. He'd wanted to ask about her, but now he didn't need to. He also didn't need to wonder why George knew so much about the whereabouts of the Yankees.

"We'll eat and sleep," George said, "and in the morning, you're gonna help me load this stuff onto a ship—I usually do business with one cap'n. Be a bunch of slaves loadin' from other plantations, and we'll just fit in. Only you'll forget to get off. Cap'n takes a crew upriver to unload. Then they truck this stuff north by wagon to Miz' Kendrick's relatives in Louisiana. Not that Louisiana ain't got the Yankees either. They been there, and they'll be back."

Noah ate two helpings of a hearty stew made with the last of winter's root vegetables and a rabbit that Martha said someone had just happened to give her. After dinner Martha made him a pallet on the floor, but Noah said he'd just as soon sleep under the stars, he was used to it. In slave quarters, it was common to sleep outside to allow a man and a woman some privacy, though Lord knows, slaves were also used to doing without it. George offered him a turn at the whiskey bottle that Martha apparently kept for him, but Noah declined. He never had developed the taste.

Noah came awake to bright daylight. Jumping out of his blanket, he was upright almost before he knew it, shaking his head. How could he have slept past daybreak? It took him a minute to realize it was night, and the day-like brightness came from fires, huge fires, that surrounded him. And he slowly realized he had been awakened as much by noise as light.

Along the shore on his side of the river, huge barrels blazed with white-hot fires. Noah recognized the smell of tar and knew what was burning. Fires also burned across the river, and Noah shielded his eyes from the light to make out skeletons of buildings, their timbers blazing before crumbling.

In the middle of the river, illuminated by the firelight, were Union ships, their gunfire providing short but intense bursts of light and noise. Guns on the bluff above him answered the Federal guns, providing their own flashes of light. To Noah, the whole world was on fire in a ghostly and frightening scene. He'd wakened in a world like nothing he'd ever seen before. He resisted the urge to run—where would he run? There was no place to get away. He put his hands over his ears but the noise penetrated, a mix of the crackling and popping of fires and the explosions of gunfire.

Behind him, he heard George say, "Looks like the end of the world, jes' like the Bible says."

"It might be the end of our world," Noah said. "Maybe the Yankees are gonna win this time."

"I don' think so," George said, turning to go back inside as though one look of the turmoil was all he wanted.

The battle, if that's what it could be called, lasted better than an hour, but then the fires began to die down, the boats disappeared, and the firing stopped. Noah tried to find sleep again in a smoky world lit now with the glow of embers, but sleep wouldn't come. Had he come this far, only to be tricked by Yankee ships and trapped in Vicksburg? His heart pounded at the thought. The ground seemed harder than it had earlier in the evening, and the air more chilly. He pulled the blanket around him.

To his surprise he was asleep when George came to wake him. It was still dark, so he couldn't see the destruction on either side of the river, but he could smell the aftermath of the fires. He splashed water on his face and hands from the pitcher that Martha had left by the door and went inside. After bowls of thick oatmeal, washed down with strong black coffee, he and George climbed into the wagon just as the sun rose. Noah made his polite thank-you to Martha, who was on her way to a house on the bluff where she cooked for a white family.

Now he could see the blackened barrels and, across the river, the ruins of three, no, four houses. The smoky smell lingered, unpleasantly mixed with morning dampness. In no time they were at the docks, and George made his way straight to the boat he wanted. "Morning," he said to the captain.

"Morning, George," the man replied, pushing a visor cap back on his head. "Quite a show last night."

"Yessir." And that was all that was said about the night's spectacle. Noah couldn't believe his ears. He wanted to talk about it, talk to erase the fiery images from his mind.

"You bring me a load?"

"Yessir, sure did. And I brought me a helper to load. This here's Adam, new to Massa Kendrick."

The captain nodded at Noah, but he would never have done more than that. Shaking hands was out of the question, and he didn't really even look at Noah, which was a relief to the runaway. The captain wouldn't recognize him on the boat. The man spoke to George. "You get started. I'll look at how much you have and get a bill ready for Kendrick."

Loading went well enough, with George calling loudly, "Careful now, boy, Miz' Kendrick sets a mighty store by that armoire. Be all billy-you-know-what to pay if we scratch it." Or, "Here, boy, watch that chair leg. It'll snap like a toothpick if you ain't careful." Noah suspected he was yelling for the captain's benefit, but he tried to be careful of the furniture. Loading was easier than fieldwork.

Slaves worked at transferring bulky boxes, more furniture, and all manner of household goods to the boat. In no time at all, the captain declared the boat was loaded as much as it could take. "Yankees keep me in business," he said, "ferrying folks' goods away from them."

George gave him a signal, and Noah slipped between the boat's railing on the offside and a stack of boxes. He hadn't even had a chance to thank George, but he supposed his thanks were understood, though unsaid. Pulling up the plank, untying from the dock, and shipping off seemed to take forever, but finally Noah heard the sound of the engine and and the steam whistle, and he felt the boat swing into the river.

He was actually leaving Mississippi. The river was between him and slave catchers, dogs, Massa Ellerbee, and all other threats—or so he thought. He'd expected relief, but he found himself trembling. The fear he'd beaten back ever since he killed Goliath now took over. Goliath! His attack on Nelly and Noah's quick move with the knife seemed a long time past, in another lifetime.

Gradually the trembling subsided, and Noah relaxed enough to look down at the river and then out across the water to the Louisiana shore. He wondered where they'd dock, how he'd get away, where he'd go.

Lost in thought he barely heard the boat captain shout, "Look alive! Union troops ahead. We're goin' back to Vicksburg. All hands on deck NOW."

Going back to Vicksburg? It couldn't be! Noah was stunned.

The boat swung toward the Louisiana shore preparing to make a wide U-turn in the river. Hardly taking a moment to think, Noah climbed the rail and dropped into the water, hoping the splash he made wouldn't be heard over the turmoil on board.

The cold water stunned him, taking his breath momentarily. He surfaced and turned toward shore. It was farther away than it had looked from the ship—much farther.

Jonah used to lecture Noah, almost scolding him into keeping his strength and determination, and now he could hear the old man's voice. "You ain't gonna die here in the water, Noah. That ain't what the good Lord intended for you. You swim, you swim for your life!"

Noah began to swim, though his swimming was at best a sort of dog paddle. He forced himself to swim slowly to save his strength. At first he swam confidently, trying to pretend that he was in the creek back at Massa Ellerbee's, back when he was a kid and didn't have to work so hard and wasn't so hungry to be free. Back when the shore was much closer than it was now.

When he first began to tire, he rolled over onto his back and floated, but that made him dizzy and frightened him because he couldn't see what was around him. So he went back to swimming. He remembered once watching, from a safe hiding place, while Massa swam in the creek, taking big long strokes and drawing the water toward him instead of the paddling that Noah did. He tried Massa's way now and found it pushed him through the water much better.

He was beginning to think he couldn't make it after all, thinking desperate thoughts, when he almost butted his head on a large, charred plank—probably from one of the houses set afire the night before. Noah grabbed it and found that he could rest on it, while still kicking his legs to push him through the water. Now the shore looked closer . . . and then closer and closer.

He was an exhausted man when he reached a tangle of brush that reached out to welcome him. He pulled himself through it and found land, only to discover he was on a finger of land, surrounded by water and covered with brush. North seemed to him the best direction to go, so he staggered ahead. Finally at long last, Noah found himself on firm ground.

He threw himself on the ground to grab a handful of dirt that was not Mississippi and to thank the Lord for bringing him to shore. And that was the last thing he remembered until he heard gruff voices above him.

"Naw, he ain't dead. I saw him move."

"Poor bastard," said a second voice.

Noah was afraid to move, afraid to look and see who stood over him. His head was too foggy to make out much about the voice, but he knew it was either a colored man or a white man like Quint, one who didn't speak proper like Massa Ellerbee . . . or Hattie Kendrick. His mind whirled. What if he opened his eyes and saw Quint? Whoever it was, he was at their mercy.

They wore blue uniforms.

Chapter Three
by Carlton Stowers

Before being jolted awake by the kick to his rib cage, Noah had been lost in a dream unlike any he'd ever had before. On warm nights back on Massa Ellerbee's plantation, when sheer exhaustion from the sunrise-to-sundown field work finally yielded to restless sleep, the visions that invaded his attempt at rest were always the same: the imagined lashes from the whip, Goliath's foul breath in his face, even the salty taste of blood in his mouth when a nightmare fist would smash against his face. So intense were the little mind plays, so real the pain, that he would wake, soaked in sweat, shivering, relieved to recognize the familiar night sounds from the row of slave shanties. Only then would his fear of the dark hours subside as he lay listening to a baby's cry and the gentle song of a mother offering comfort. Even the faraway barking of the plantation hounds on their moonlit hunts briefly eased the anxiety. Until the sleep his tired body demanded would finally return, taking him back to the ugly and cruel scenes that paraded through his subconscious.

On this night, after painfully making his way to the shelter of the brush and damp weeds, every muscle aching from the swim to shore, the still-fresh wounds on his back a throbbing reminder of his reason for his insanely dangerous run for freedom, he had begged God for only a few hours of peaceful rest. Empty of spirit and hope, he could not summon even the slightest will to contemplate what might lie ahead in the days to come.

* * *

If death was to be the ultimate result of his folly, he would just as soon it not be slow in coming. It was his last thought—a prayer, really—before closing his eyes and fading into an exhausted sleep.

And with the sleep came the dream. And in the dream, the warm and soft image of Nelly.

They were seated at a table back at Jonah's cabin, a flickering candle in the center of the table casting magical shadows against the wall. Only in his dream, he hadn't been beaten. He was sitting at the table with Jonah and Aunt Suse and Nelly, and they were all happy and safe. It was as if there was no Massa Ellerbee, no Goliath.

They talked, ate sweet cornbread that Aunt Suse had warmed in lard on the small wood stove, and laughed. There was no fear, no danger lurking beyond the door, no slave catcher on the way. No ugly vision of Goliath, lying in powdery plantation dirt, bleeding and dying. In the dream, Noah had no painful whip marks crisscrossing his back. Instead of mud-caked clothing, he was cleanly dressed.

Oddly, it was as though he was a third person, looking in on and listening to the conversation that played out in his deep sleep.

"So," Nelly said, "you'll be going to Texas, will you?"

"Reckon so. If I can figger me a way to make it in one piece. Not real sure the trip's gonna be worth it, though. What I hear is there ain't much any place safe for colored folks. Here or Texas. Or anywheres in between."

"And just what you hear?"

"That's they's only bad and worse folks waiting out there, fighting this war. Soldiers in the South, they want to make sure nothing changes. They're fightin' to hold their ground and see that us niggers are kept slaves. Them Yankees from up north, even if they win, ain't likely to want to change that."

In Noah's dream, Nelly smiled as she picked a small corner from her slice of cornbread and reached across the table to place it in his mouth. "Might not be all as bad as you think, Noah," she said. "Jes' maybe be better days coming."

"And what makes ya'll think that?"

Nelly shrugged and smiled, as if she knew some secret.

It didn't matter that she gave him no answer. In this dream moment, his only wish was for Nelly to continue talking, her soft voice spreading a warmth over him he'd never before known.

She reached across the table to brush her hand against his. "You're big and strong. And Lord knows you got some hardheaded determination. I 'spect one of these days you just might do yourself real proud," he heard her say.

* * *

The sudden searing pain in his side woke him. Immediately gone was the image of Nelly and the lyrical sound of her voice. Noah gritted his teeth and clutched a clump of nearby cattails in an effort to keep from screaming. From what seemed like miles away he heard a growling voice.

"If'n you're alive, boy, best you get on your feet and let us have a look at you."

Dizzy with the new pain, Noah slowly lifted his head and first saw the scruffed and muddy boot that had delivered the blow to his ribs, then tattered blue pants, and finally the bearded face of the first Union soldier he'd ever seen.

He had managed to pull himself into a kneeling position, his knees sinking in the ooze of the soggy river bottom, when the man standing over him spoke again. "You one of them runaway slave niggers, ain'tcha?"

When Noah didn't answer, the man quickly raised the rifle he was carrying. It was at that moment that Noah was vaguely aware of a second soldier. "Aw, come on, Bear," he yelled, "ain't no call to kill him. Looks like he's done half dead anyways. If he can find a way to walk, let's take him back to camp and figger out if he's worth keeping."

Noah didn't wait to be asked. "I kin walk," he said, his pained voice little more than a whisper. "I kin walk jes' fine."

* * *

During the next several days he would have no memory of the pre-dawn hike to the well-hidden Union camp, of being placed on a blanket inside a small, darkened tent. There was no memory of the beans and cornbread and coffee regularly fed to him, only foggy awareness of constant activity nearby.

Finally fully awake, he lifted himself onto one elbow and peered through the small tent opening, wary of what new challenge awaited him beyond the safety of his hiding place. The smoke of a half dozen campfires drifted lazily into a clear midday sky and soldiers were hurrying about. An army camp. What was most unreal about the scene he was viewing was the sight of black faces mingled among the whites. A couple of colored women were tending a fire over which a huge cauldron of something that smelled wonderful was cooking. Men were stacking wood nearby. Two more were watering several hobbled horses.

"Well, hidy-do," he heard a man say. "Looks like ol' Lazarus' done finally risen. I'd about give up hope you was coming back to the living."

Noah gave the elderly black man a puzzled look. "Where am I?"

"Not much for formalities are you, son? My name's John B. Scobell, but folks mostly jus' call me Preacher John. Who would you be?"

"I'm Noah. Jus' Noah." Then he repeated, "Where am I?"

"Glad to know you, Jus' Noah. You are now in the company of a regiment of fightin' Union army soldiers what's busy trying to run the evil Confederates out of the town of Vicksburg over yonder on the other side of the river. You do still got enough of your senses to know there's a war a'goin' on. . . ."

Noah stared at the old man whose skin stretched tightly over a frame that seemed all bone and sharp angles, his hair and beard the color of the summer cotton he'd picked for Massa Ellerbee since boyhood. In his visitor's gnarled hands were two tin cups. On his face was a smile.

"I ain't gone crazy," Noah finally replied, feeling easier about the man with whom he was talking, the man he assumed had nursed him back to health. "Jes' got a little beat up and tired out."

"Happens when a feller's on the run, I reckon."

"I'd be pleased to know what kind o' mess I done got myself into," Noah said as he tried to sit.

* * *

His knowledge of the world was limited, bound by the fence lines of the plantation where he'd lived for as long as he could remember. Like all others who slaved under the stern eye of Old Man Ellerbee, he could neither read nor write. From time to time he'd heard stories of faraway places where slavery didn't exist and coloreds were even allowed to go to school, but wasn't sure he believed them. More than likely, he was convinced, such tales were just wishes of how things might be rather than the true facts of the matter.

Noah knew little about the war he had fled into, only that folks in the southern states were putting up a fight for the right to mind their own business and keep their slaves working their plantations. Up north, however, a man named President Lincoln had said the colored folks had the right to be free.

"Some of it makes sense, some of it don't," Preacher John explained as he offered a cup filled with hot, bile-tasting chicory coffee.

"First thing you need know is that even if you've done distanced yourself from your owner, you still got enemies everywhere. That said, the white folks here ain't as bad as those they's fighting on the other side of the river. The coloreds you see here have seen the light and chose their side, me along with them. You'd be right smart to do the same, if you ask me. Which, o' course, you ain't done yet."

And with that Preacher John told Noah the story of a nation at war.

He talked of a place Noah had never heard of—Fort Sumter up in South Carolina—where the fighting had begun, then told of how it had quickly moved southward. He told of a large numbers of colored men and boys up north who were volunteering to fight alongside the Union soldiers. "What I hear is the white folk, they don't want them, fearing they're too dumb or cowardly to fight proper, but the coloreds keep trying to sign up anyways. Word is they's already been some with light enough skin who've done joined. My guess is the time's coming when the North's soon gonna let them all in on the fightin'. I 'spect that's what its gonna take to get this war settled and won. And the colored soldiers is gettin' ready, organizing and training, anxious to get themselves a uniform and a gun. I hear they's thousands. Ready and waitin'.

"Me, I'm from New Orleans. Worked for a massa down there even tho' I wadn't no slave, thanks to the fact I got some French blood pumping in my ol' veins. You see, when the French give the Louisiana Territory to the United States, part of the signed deal was that any colored folks what had French or Spanish in their blood had to be allowed they freedom. So I worked as a houseboy and did a little Sunday preaching. 'Course I got no papers saying I'm a true preacher, but I got me a Bible. And I can read it a bit. And, as you probably done figgered, I don't mind talking.

"By the time the war come down here, everthing had got plumb crazy. Here, you had Union soldiers fightin' to set colored folks free—and damned—pardon my language—if they wadn't a whole bunch of slave boys who up and took sides with them ol' Confederates.

"Didn't make no sense to me, so I done the same thing you done. Free or not, I took off running to some place I could feel a mite safer. This here's as far as I got."

He told of how the slaves who had started out helping the South quickly changed sides once they saw that the Yankee soldiers were winning. "Like I say, don't all of this play out real smart. Least not to me."

"You a soldier now?"

"Oh, no, ain't none of us real soldiers. That ain't allowed by decree of the war commander up north. This here's a white man's fight, plain and simple. We's only here to help out. But it ain't all that bad."

Noah gave the man a confused look.

"See, the law, it says that if the Union captures runaways, they's supposed to return 'em to they owners. Now, I ask you, does that make good reason? Them fighting to get slaves freed and all but still bein' ordered to send 'em right back to where they come from?

"Anyways, they's a lot of Yankee soldiers think that's plumb crazy and choose to ignore it. Thank the blessed Lord, I might add. The man in charge here, he's of that mind."

He then told a tale that Noah found difficult to believe.

Not long after he'd arrived in the Union camp, Preacher John said, a slave catcher had come in search of a runaway. "The boy was here, a'course, but Colonel Abernathy—he's the one's in charge of this regiment—hid him away in one of the soldier tents.

"Polite and accommodating as all get-out, he escorted the catcher man through the camp, allowing him to look wherever he pleased. But when they come to the tent where the runaway was hiding, the colonel explained that one of his men was inside, dying of the fever and smallpox. 'Course, wasn't nobody wanting to poke their head in there and get themselves sick too, so they passed that tent right on by.

"Once he was convinced his boy wasn't nowhere in the camp, the man shook the colonel's hand, gentleman-like as you please, and rode off. The runaway, he finally peeked out of the tent, grinning like you wouldn't believe, and went to work."

"What kind of work would that be?" Noah asked.

"'Bout anything needs doing," Preacher John replied. "Other than soldiering. The coloreds cook and unload supply wagons. They's a few womenfolk here, they do washing and mending. The men, they chop the wood to keep the fires burning. Care for the horses. And dig latrines. And, when need be, graves for those unfortunates kilt in battle. On occasion Colonel Abernathy even asks me to say a few words 'fore the deceased is put to rest.

"We don't get no thirteen dollar payday like the soldiers, but we get our beans and cornbread regular and a blanket to sleep on. Like I say, all in all this ain't no bad place to be right now.

"But they's something you wanna think on right hard 'fore you walk out of this tent: Don't never be lettin' your guard down. Mixed in with the kindly folks are some that's meaner 'n a water snake. Don't go gettin' it in your head that you got friends here." And then he smiled and extended his hand, ". . . lessen' you wanna count ol' Preacher John."

Despite the warning, to Noah it all sounded better than anything he'd ever heard of, certainly an improvement on life back at Massa Ellerbee's plantation. Preacher John had made no mention of anybody getting whipped or chained up and drug behind a mule or hanged by the neck. As he listened, his thoughts retreated to his dream of Nelly and in his mind he could again hear her gentle whisper. *Things might not be all as bad as you think, Noah.*

* * *

He was surprised at how quickly his strength returned. Soon he was doing his day's work alongside the other colored men, chopping and digging, feeling new life return to his muscles. There was no overseer standing watch, no threats of harm if he didn't work harder or faster. When thirsty, he stopped to drink whenever he pleased.

It amazed him that some men were even sent riding off on mules, free as air, to scout for berries and wild onions and pokeweed greens so the women would have something to cook with the game brought into camp by the soldiers.

Still, Noah kept a wary eye on all about him. Except for an occasional nod to Preacher John at mealtime or a few words with his new friend at night before spreading his blanket on a far corner of camp, he spoke to no one, colored folk or white soldiers. So long as he had an ax or a shovel in his hand, he soon decided, he'd be left alone. It was a relief to him that the soldiers, busy with the work of their war, ignored him.

The battle across the river had turned into a seemingly endless siege as the stubborn Confederates held their ground, reinforced by new troops that were arriving daily from throughout Mississippi. With Vicksburg being a crucial river gateway, both sides understood its importance to the ultimate outcome of the war. If the Yankees were to win, it was imperative they have the freedom to navigate their supply boats up and down the big, winding river.

Day and night, the distant echo of cannon and musket fire could be heard. And when soldiers wearily returned to camp for food and rest, their faces were grim, their eagerness for battle clearly fading. As the fighting stretched on, more and more dead were returned to camp, their limp and bloodied bodies tethered to their horses.

Helping dig graves filled much of Noah's work time.

Some Yankee soldiers simply didn't return at all. "They done had all the fightin' they want," Preacher John explained, "and skeedaddled. They're headin' home, their lives now no better'n yours. They get caught for desertin', they'll be shot by their own. But, I guess it don't matter who kills you once you got it in your mind you don't want to be fightin' no more. Like I tol' you, don't all this make a whole lotta sense."

* * *

In truth, many of those who had taken up arms for the Yankee cause had not done so out of any sense of real patriotism or eagerness to help reunite the nation or to see that colored people were given their rightful due. Times were hard back home, and the Federal payday had been their incentive. It was as simple as that. Such had been the case with Bear Coltrain, the soldier who had happened upon Noah on the riverbank weeks earlier. Back home in Virginia, he'd failed at farming and had finally resorted to stealing from his neighbors simply to keep food on the table for his wife and babies. Occasionally, he'd earn a dollar by winning a drunken boxing match on the town square against some misguided opponent who had little chance against his massive frame and powerful fists. Mean and mad at the hand the world had dealt him, Bear had enlisted in the Union army and fled Virginia without so much as even telling his wife he was leaving. Fighting, he told himself, was what he did best.

But, now, he too had reached the conclusion that soldiering was just another in his long, tired litany of mistakes. "Done had me 'bout all this I reckon I want," he said one late night as he sat gazing into the embers of a campfire. "Seems to me this here war's gonna go on forever, or at least till we all wind up getting ourselves kilt."

Three other soldiers, blankets draped over their hunched shoulders, nodded in agreement as they silently poked sticks at the fire. They, too, were tired and homesick and regretful of their decision to join in the war. They hated the hot days and cold nights, the bugs that nipped at their necks and left huge welts, the sores on their feet, caused by the mud and river water that seeped into their boots. And, while none would admit it, they were scared.

Finally, the youngest of the group spoke up. "Seems to me we got ourselves backed into a bad corner. We keep on fighting in hopes one day it gets over and we're still alive and in one piece. Or we high-tail it and be looked on as a coward deserter."

"Damned if you do, damned if you don't," another said.

"I ain't no coward," Bear said. "I just got me some sense. I been figgerin' on me a plan."

Already, he whispered, he'd made up his mind that he would soon steal a horse and head back to Virginia. He would take one of the runaway slaves with him. At worst, if he encountered other Union soldiers during his flight, he would be able to explain that he was on a mission, given orders to return the slave to his rightful owner. At best, he'd find some plantation owner or some slave catcher along the way who was eager to have his hostage for a figure that far exceeded army pay.

Impressed by Bear's plan, the others again nodded. The way soldiers had been disappearing on a daily basis, it was unlikely he would even be missed until he was long gone.

"If I'm real lucky," he grinned, showing his tobacco-stained teeth, "folks'll just figger I got shot dead and my horse run away."

"Which nigger you figgerin' on takin'?"

"I'm taking one what's young and strong, one that'll bring me a right smart price once I find me a buyer. The one I got my eye on is that young buck we pulled out of the weeds down yonder at the river a while back. I been keeping my eye on him. He's strong as an ox and works without pause. My guess is he might fetch a hundred dollars or more."

In a nearby grove of trees, well beyond the flickering last glow of the campfire, Preacher John squatted, barely breathing as he listened to the soldiers' conversation. He'd been awakened by the call of nature that had begun routinely to interrupt his sleep and, since the latrine designated for the coloreds was on the opposite side of the camp, he'd taken to tending his nocturnal business in the privacy of the woods.

"When you doin' this?" he heard one of the soldiers ask.

"Right soon," Bear replied as he poured the sour remains from his coffee cup onto the dying coals. "Right soon."

* * *

Noah was wakened by a hand firmly clutched across his mouth. He struggled briefly before his eyes adjusted to the moonless darkness and saw that the man kneeling over him was Preacher John.

"Shhh, boy. Jes' lay right still and listen real careful to what it is I got to tell you." He removed his bony hand from Noah's mouth and placed it gently on his bare shoulder. And told him of the conversation he'd overheard just an hour earlier.

"I had to wait till I was sure they was sleeping before I could come and warn you. My thinking," he said, "is you best get yourself going. Quick as you can."

Without a word, Noah was already hitching up his britches and reaching for his worn-out pair of boots. His mind raced as he contemplated his escape and life back on the run.

Preacher John watched in silence for a several seconds, then asked, "What is it you 'spect on finding over yonder in Texas?"

"What I hear is they got a whole lot of space."

"I reckon that's as good a reason as any. A man can run and hide till his heart's content . . . or plumb wears out. Which ever comes first."

"I best be going so I can get as far as I can 'fore daylight."

Preacher John held up a sack filled with cornbread and biscuits. "We'll be needing this," he whispered.

He allowed Noah no time to argue. "I'm figgerin' on goin' with you. Don't go worrying. If I fall behind, you can go ahead on without me, though I 'spect it'll be you trying to keep up since the Lord saw fit to bless me with a good ration of strength and will."

Sitting there in the pitch darkness, the only certainty of his future the new dangers that awaited, Noah spoke. "You run with me, you're jes' asking for trouble you ain't even considered. What I ain't told you is I done killed a man. And, if need be, I'll likely kill me some more if that be what it takes. I got nothing to lose."

Preacher John smiled broadly. "The man you're talking about, he need killing?"

"I reckon he did, long 'fore I got it done."

"Then, they's two things you ought to know. First, I got no cause to judge what you done."

"What's the other?"

"I ain't never seen Texas and would rightly admire to do so," the preacher said.

* * *

Miles away, on the rocky edge of a Mississippi creek bed, Quint watched as his horse carefully made its way to drink. Nearby, the tethered mules ridden by his sleeping sons stood motionless. Fearful that a campfire might call unwanted attention to their presence, slave catcher sat in the darkness, wishing for coffee but instead he reached into his pouch and stuffed another chaw of tobacco into his mouth.

Staring into the swift-running water, his horses' hooves clicking against the smooth rocks the only sound, Quint had but one thought in mind. It had been there since he'd ridden away from Ellerbee's place weeks earlier. Focused on his mission, he wasn't likely to eat or sleep much until it was accomplished. No runaway slave was going to show him up by evading capture. He'd stay on that bad nigger Noah's track for years, if that's what it took.

From beneath the shelter of a nearby willow, his oldest son stirred, sat up and willed his eyes to focus on the nearby figure.

"Paw," Quint Two whispered, "ya'll okay?"

Quint spat a chocolate spray of tobacco juice in the direction of the creek, not bothering to wipe away that which dripped down his chin. "Will be," he replied, "soon as I find me that nigger Noah and kill him dead."

Chapter Four

by Phyllis Allen

"Lord, please make this man go before I kill him."

The brown-skinned woman with green eyes stretched her body upward from the straw of the stable floor. Closing her eyes she mouthed the prayer again, "Lord, please make this man leave me alone."

The man advanced, cursing loudly, and raised his arm in a threatening gesture. "You're just about the stupidest, clumsiest, and most ignorant black gal I ever did see. You ain't got the brains it would take to make a hummingbird fly. I'd beat you, but you just ain't worth the effort it would take. You're triflin' like ever other woman and nigger I ever seen."

He never saw the knife that silently etched a smile beneath his chin. By the time the red reached from his left ear to his right, he had stopped breathing.

Wiping the steel blade on the rough hem of her dress, she slid the knife into its leather scabbard, and it disappeared into the darkness of the canvas bag she carried.

She reached forward and with her outstretched hand closed the icy blue eyes with her fingertips just as she had watched Lil' Missy do the day Overseer Bailes beat the slave Cato to death at the request of Massa Burwell. She didn't bother to kiss his rapidly-bluing lips as Lil' Missy did.

Standing, she took one quick look around the stall and backed out—right into the rock-hard arms of a man. Whirling around, ready to do battle, Lovie froze as her green eyes locked onto a matching pair of eyes.

Shocked, Noah said, "Lovie, can that be you?"

The woman stared a long time, eyebrows knit together in puzzlement. Then a smile split her thin, troubled face. She said, "Oh, my God, is that you, Noah? My brother Noah that I thought was dead?"

"Yep, it's me, and it's a good thing I'm not some kin of that man you killed. Damn, Lovie, you know who that is?" Noah craned his neck to look over Lovie's shoulder at the man stretched out on the floor of the stall.

"I reckon I do. I killed him, didn't I?" she said. "Quick! You got a horse? I'll tell you all about it on our way out of here."

Noah grabbed his horses' reins and asked, "What you doin' in Texas? How did you get here in the first place and where you headed, Lovie?"

"Anywhere that he ain't," Lovie jerked her head in the dead man's direction.

After they'd mounted the horses and ridden some distance away from the barn, Noah asked, "So you gonna tell me what you doin' with these white folks and how you happened to kill Quint Carpenter's favorite son?"

"Remember down in Noxubee County, Mississippi? Remember how Massa Burwell called Mama a dumb, ignorant nigger all the time? Then he hit her cross her back with that board, remember?"

"I do, but I am surprised that you do. You couldn't have been taller than that," he said indicating the off the side of his horse.

"Mama was a hard woman to forget. I remember how she screamed and screamed and tore her clothes when Massa Burwell sold you off. Sometimes it be late at night, I be alone and I hear Mama screamin', screamin', and screamin' till I have to put my hands over my ears so I don't hear no more."

Noah looked behind them, worrying that some of Quint Carpenter's men might appear in the distance. He said to Lovie, "That's funny. I remember how Mama used to save us biscuits and a chicken leg from Massa's table. I remember how her hair was thick and soft just like wool. I remember how her arms felt when she hugged you real close to her chest, but I ain't never remembered her screamin' till today."

"Well, she did scream and that screamin' is kinda why Massa Ben Carpenter is layin' back there dead."

Noah looked at her with his forehead wrinkled in confusion.

"Massa Ben, he sells horses and steals 'em too sometimes. Came through Mississippi and traded some horses for me. Mama be gone by then, so I didn't have to hear her screamin'. Man had told us about the 'mancipation but Massa Burwell, he took them horses anyway."

"Lovie! Can't nobody trade for you now. You're free."

"I know that, but that don't mean that white folks can't do what they wants to do with me. You too. We may be free 'cause some man come with a piece of paper, sat on a horse, and read out loud to all of us gathered 'round. Sayin' all of them wherefores, withouts, and what ifs don't make a people free."

"Look at me. I ain't got no master. Nobody tells Noah Freeman what to do. Nobody."

"That's 'cause you a man. Black as you is, you still a man. You know what that means?"

Still looking behind them, Noah said, "Means I worked in the fields from way before sunup till way after sundown and got whipped with the lash when I couldn't."

"Yeah, men got it hard, but not like no woman. A woman ain't got no say about her life, her children, nothin'. That's the way of the world. That's what Massa Ben used to say."

"So you still ain't told me why you killed him."

Now Lovie was looking back to be sure nobody was behind them. Then she said, "Like I said, he come and took me from Mississippi. First he played like he wanted to take me so I can be a nursemaid to his children, be a helper to his wife. Ain't got no wife and no children. He dragged me from one camp to another followin' work crews and soldiers. 'Stead of sellin' horses, he was sellin' me."

Noah winced, as if she had slapped him, "You should have left him."

"I tried."

Pulling down the rough muslin of her dress Lovie revealed a mangled mass of muscles, scars, and pink puckers where her right breast should have been.

"He did that to you?"

"That ain't the worst thing he done to me. It just the only thing I can show you."

"Lovie, I'm sorry."

"Massa Ben took me from camp to camp. But that ain't what made it bad. All of them men don't mean nothin', but he never called me nothin' but ox, mule, dumb, triflin', lazy, good-for-nothin', ignorant— all the names that make your head too heavy to hold up. I let him do it and didn't say a word. This time I can't let him call me no more names. It's just too hard. I just prayed to God don't let me kill him, make him leave me alone.

"Noah, you ain't gon' want to hear this and you can't understand it, but I all Massa Ben got. His daddy mean as a snake and never taught him nothing but how to be mean and low down too. He weren't always mean though. When we was alone sometimes he be different. He lay his head in my lap and he cry 'bout how his daddy beat his mama to death and how, ever since he ain't felt no love. He be scared sometimes too, but then he git full of likker. I can't let him call me no more names. It jes' too hard. I prayed to God to don't let me kill him."

Noah said, "Well I guess that's a prayer that went unanswered."

"Yeah," she said grimly as they bounced over the rough uneven trail putting distance between themselves and the corpse that lay behind them in the barn on the edge of the community of Fort Worth. It wasn't more than ten miles to the little ranch that Noah Freeman and his wife Nelly were trying to make a go of in North Texas, but it seemed a long ride that day.

Lovie said, "You think Massa Ben's daddy goin' to come lookin' for me?"

Noah, who knew how Quint Carpenter thought, said, "Ain't no question about that. He be looking for me too when he finds out that you and me share blood. He sure goin' to come lookin' to spill some of it."

By the time pink started to streak the blackness of the sky, they slowed at a rough, wooden gate, obviously handmade.

"This is it," Noah said proudly.

"What?"

"This is Free Land, my piece of Texas. House was standin' here when I found the place, not in bad shape. I fixed it up some."

Lovie saw a board cabin that reminded her strangely of the slave cabins back in Mississippi. Its mud-and-stone fireplace was almost straight, but the roof slanted to one side and there looked to be new caulking between some of the boards. But the porch had a fresh coat of paint, and someone had planted something small and green in front of the house. It was, she thought, a house where folks tried, they really tried.

"Noah, can't no black man own land in Texas," Lovie protested.

"I sure can," he said. "This place's called Mosier Valley. Yonder's the Trinity River. Mosiers owned a plantation and when they freed their slaves, they gave them this land. Rest of us bought a bit, so we got our own community here."

"Where'd you get money to buy land?" she asked suspiciously.

"I saved this white officer, Captain Malone, one time—southern soldier about to ambush him. So he helped me buy this. I'll pay him off soon. I got a good crop of cotton, and Nelly, she's raisin' vegetables for our table. Sometimes I do a little work for white folks around. I ain't pickin' their cotton, but I can do handywork. Even Massa Ellerbee used to say I was always handy." He grinned proudly.

Halfway up the road that led to the house Noah stopped. Turning to Lovie, he spread his arm expressively, "This is my land, over to that stand of trees. It belongs to me. Well, to me and Nelly." He stared thoughtfully at the trees. "Lovie, you don't know how good it feels to own land."

She turned and looked at the land, with its planted rows of cotton and its scrubby trees. And then she looked at her brother and saw his grin. And she grinned too.

They rode the short distance to the cabin. As they lowered themselves from the horses and started to tie them up, the door of the ranch opened and a woman appeared, hugely pregnant in spite of her small frame.

The woman said, "Noah, thought you was goin' to be gone for two days."

"Things happened. Meet my sister, Lovie. She was taken by Ben Carpenter, Quint the slave catcher's son. It's been hard times for her, but she just sent him to his permanent rest. So now me and Lovie on the run from Quint, and I had to hotfoot it back here and try to hide her."

Nelly accepted the news matter of factly. Violence had been part of her life for so long that it didn't unnerve her. "Well come on inside," she said. "It's too cold to be standin' out here, and Miz Lovie ain't dressed for no cold."

"I'll be in directly. Got to take care of the horses."

"Miz Nelly, I am pleased to meet you. That lunkhead brother of mine ain't said that I had no sister. Look like you 'bout to have a young'un too," Lovie palmed Nelly's stomach and stroked it slowly.

Nelly smiled, "We already got us two boys, and this one I'm hopin' to be a sweet baby girl. I'm tired of being the only gal on the place. And now with you here, I got grownup female company."

Noah stood to the side with a big grin splitting his face as he watched the two women embrace.

Later, over fresh baked biscuits, ham, and strong black coffee the three exchanged stories as two wide-eyed young boys sat by the fireplace listening.

"Miz Nelly, how you meet up with this brother of mine?"

Nelly said, "Was before the emancipation. I was on the Ellerbee plantation and Noah . . . he saved me from Massa's big buck Goliath. He killed that bad nigger and had to run away. But I didn't never forget him, and I made up my mind to find him if it took the rest of my life. After emancipation when everybody tryin' to walk to find them some freedom, me and most the folks from Ellerbee's plantation got on the road with 'em."

Nelly got a far-off look in her eyes as she remembered crossing the Mississippi into Louisiana with the help of some Union soldiers and then walking westward all across Louisiana, a trip that took the better part of a year. There were fifty of the ex-slaves when they started out toward Texas.

"Some of the old folks and a few of the children died on the way to Texas. So did Jessup's mama, Hagar, and that's when I promised her I'd raise him." She put a hand on the head of the oldest boy. "But we kept finding ex-slaves like us who was working free on their old massa's plantations. Lots of 'em took us in and fed us. We even picked cotton with 'em to make a little money to keep us on the road to Texas."

Lovie marveled at Nelly's story, "And none of them white folks in Louisiana tried to rape you?"

"Oh, some of them did, but they was so many of us that we could keep them off till we moved on.

"Well, we finally made it to a town called Marshall in East Texas, and there I heard of a big ex-slave called Noah that was ridin' with some Yankee cavalry officer and headed for a town called Fort Worth. I prayed it might be my Noah."

Nelly rocked and remembered how hard the trek had been. Lovie thought the whole story had been told, and, looking across the room, she smiled at the two toast-colored children, "They some right fine boys, Sister Nelly."

"Boys, say thank you to your Auntie Lovie. This is Noah, Jr. and Jessup, Miz Lovie," Nelly looked at both boys and smiled at their shy "thank you ma'ams."

"Both of you most welcome," their new aunt said.

"Anyways, Miz Lovie, finally, we was mostly some women and babies comin' west. The men done run off or been taken for soldiers. Ol' Uncle Jonah was goin' to find his wife that got sold off when they was young. Never made it though—he died 'fore we was into Texas. We was down to our last food and didn't know which way to go. There was some river was in front of us. Don't recollect the name. Seemed like we crossed about a thousand rivers and creeks on our way here. We begged rides on boats and paid to catch ferries. One or two we even had to swim for it. We were camped on the bank of this one and didn't know how we was going to get across. For the first time since we had left I was thinking that maybe it wasn't so bad at Massa's place. We was fed good mostly and didn't hardly get beat, 'less we didn't work or did some devilment. While I was thinkin' what to do, I went down to the river to fetch some water, and there was Noah with his glass-green eyes."

Noah was back in the room when Nelly had told about finding him. He laughed and said, "Yep. There she was, the girl with sad eyes that I remembered from Massa Ellerbee's and all the beatings I got there. She always nursed me, and she'd been haunting my dreams. I couldn't help but ask her what was wrong."

"He shore did. I looked right at him and started cryin'. Me. Watched them sell my mama and two brothers away and ain't cried. Even when my granny coughed her life away I never cried. But, I take one look at your brother, and the tears start flowin' just like that river."

"She cried so hard it scared me. I thought maybe she was scared of me or something," his voice trailed off as one of his sons climbed into his lap.

"When I stopped cryin' I told him about our group and how we were tryin' to find freedom, but we were sick and dyin' and lost. Glory to God! That ol' green-eye man climbed down off that horse and helped me fetch the water, opened his saddlebag, and shared his food. Then he went somewhere, came back with a wagon. I ain't knowed 'bout no kind of love between a man and a woman but I knows I don't want that green-eye man to go nowhere away from me."

"She didn't know that I wasn't plannin' on goin' nowhere. I had already seen that she had them good wide birthin' hips," Noah grinned and ducked as his wife swatted at him.

"He brought me and all those folks here to his place and helped me nurse them back to health. Aunt Suse and the others wanted to go back toward Louisiana—they said there was more of their own kind in East Texas. Ain't many black folk out here, 'cept those in this valley. I stayed right here, didn't need no one but Noah. Ain't no massa, just me and my husband. He is my husband. We had a weddin' with a preacher, a piece of paper, and everything. Our boys are growin' up free. We done built a decent life."

Nelly and Noah's hands met in the center of the rough-hewn table.

Lovie leaned forward, looking into the pools of green that so nearly matched her own. "Noah what happened to you after Old Massa sold you away?"

"They hooked me to that slave train, and we was goin' down to the Mississippi Delta to work in the cotton fields. Sold me to Massa Ellerbee, and it was there I run away from. There was this big, mean field hand, name of Goliath that Nelly told you 'bout. Massa made him do all of his dirty work. Me an' him got into a tussle one day he was gonna take advantage of Nelly, like she said. I tried to stop him and next thing you know, Goliath dead. I know that Massa ain't goin' to take kindly to me killin' his top nigger, so I left runnin'. Ran right into the Yankees and threw in with them."

"You was a soldier?"

"More like a mule or a field hand with no field to work."

"You fight in the war?"

"I had to run from the first bunch of Yankee soldiers I fell in with. One of 'em planned to desert, make me come with him and sell me later on. But then I met some raiders led by Captain Malone and joined up with them. Carried messages, helped scout, and saved the captain's life once. Then finally the war was over. The emancipation done come, and I set out to be free. That's why I named myself Freeman so I won't never again be without freedom."

"If you is Freeman, guess that's makes me Freelady, since I'm your sister. I like that, Lovie Free Lady." She paused a minute and then asked, "How'd you get all the way to Texas?"

"Coming to Texas was Preacher John's dream. I met Preacher John when I got with the Yankees the first time. He's the best friend I ever had, and he's the one that married us. We rode together all during the war and always planned to have us a cattle ranch in Texas when the freedom come—and we did. But, thanks to Bear Coltrain and Quint Carpenter, of course, he can't stay 'round here. Preacher John is working with some folks back in East Texas, protecting colored families from the nightriders. He keeps in touch with us though, and if we need him, he'll be right here."

"I know Quint Carpenter, only too well," Lovie said. "But who's Bear Coltrain?"

"Lovie, he's the Yankee soldier I was telling about, one of the meanest sumbitches since Lucifer walked the earth. Wanted to kidnap me from the army and sell me again for a slave, but Preacher John helped me get away. The other you know about—Quint Carpenter and his two mangy sons, Quint Two and Ben, the one what you killed. They're mean ol' boar hogs and just looking for someone, me mostly, to do harm to. Quint wanted the reward Massa Ellerbee offered on me—and the chance to kill me. Ain't no reward any more, but I 'spect he'd still like to kill me. He knows where I am, and he and his find ways to remind me they're just waiting for their chance to finish me off. Hurt Quint's pride that he never caught up to me before the war was over and I was free.

"Last year, right after I picked my cotton, Quint Two burnt my barn down to the ground—with all that cotton in it. I didn't have no crop to sell. Would have burnt the house too, but I got that put that out before it burnt all the way. Old man Quint done got himself elected to be county sheriff, and his son, Quint Two, is his deputy. That's why Ben brought you here—his daddy and brother are the law in this part of North Texas. Ain't nobody watching over what they do. Bear Coltrain, he owns a ranch yonder and wants all this land in the valley. But he reckons to start with me and my place. I'm 'fraid you killin' Ben done made things a whole lot harder. Law in Fort Worth might help us, but they don't reach out here."

"How Quint get to so much power?" Lovie asked. "He weren't nothin' but a slave catcher."

"He sldes up to the carpetbaggers that be runnin' the state these days," Noah said. "I don't know what he done for them—money, women, liquor—who knows? But they got him in as sheriff, and ain't nothin' we can do about it right now."

Lovie looked at the two boys and said, "I'll go. Can't bring no harm to you and yours 'cause of my foolishness."

"Naw, Lovie, you can't go. I been lookin' for you for a long time. It's no accident our paths crossed when they did. When I heard from some cowhand 'bout the colored woman in town got green eyes just like mine, I went in and tried to look, wanted to see if it was you. I kept asking folks 'bout this woman with green eyes. One of them drovers told me that the woman I was lookin' for was workin' down in the cribs by the cattle pens and stable. Ever' night I stand out there in the darkness watchin' them men come and go. Saw Massa Ben take their money. I come in the day-time today 'cause I thought I might find you without Massa Ben. If it turned out you were my sister, I planned to beg you to stay here with me and Nelly. I brung the horse with me in case I could get you away from here without gettin' killed myself."

"You saw me?"

"Mostly I just heard you, but it ain't no matter," Noah said.

"Nelly know what I done?"

"Me and Nelly mostly tells each other everything," he said and looked at his wife.

"We done all been made to do things we ain't wanted to. I just glad you made it home, Sister," Nelly said. She had gone to the put the boys to bed and come back into the room so quietly that neither Lovie nor Noah noticed her.

None of them heard the horses. It was the flash of light and the fire from the torch thrown into the house that brought them to their feet.

A voice came from the yard, "Nigger, git out here."

The flames were licking at the homespun muslin curtains that framed the window. Picking up the straw broom, Noah beat out the flames and at the same time pushed his wife, sister, and the two little boys into the room behind him, "Stay down. No matter what you hear out there don't come out till they gone." Then he was gone from their sight.

Crouching in the corner farthest away from the front room Nelly clutched the two whimpering children to her. Lovie stood with her back pressed flat against the wall and peeked around the doorframe. Noah was kneeling by the side of the still smoldering window with a shotgun in his calloused hands. The men outside had stopped hollering and were trying to entice the occupants of the house with quiet words.

"Noah, Noah Freeman, you and your family come outside. We just want to talk to you. There's things that need to be talked out."

"Noah, this here's Bear, Bear Coltrain. Come on out now. I guarantee that ain't nobody out here gonna hurt you or none of y'all in there. Quint is a little upset. He's got to bury his son. Boy found dead this morning down in the stables in town. Throat cut from ear to ear, some nigger gal he was tryin' to be friendly to. Somebody said you was in town askin' 'bout a green-eyed nigger woman. Thought maybe you might know where she can be found. Come on out now."

"Mr. Coltrain. Nobody here but me and my family. Don't mean no disrespect to you or Mr. Quint, but Massa Ben wasn't really the type to befriend a woman, specially a colored one."

"Boy, what you sayin'? You know somethin' 'bout my boy's death. I'll burn you, your woman, and them pickaninnies if you don't get out here right now."

"No sir, Mr. Quint, right now it be better if you go on back into town and I come in later. We can talk back in . . . ."

"Nigger, you get your black ass out here right now."

"Daddy, don't talk no more," one of the men said.

The shotgun blast shattered the glass pane that Noah had sent for all the way to Kansas City.

Lovie slid gracefully around the corner of the door, and before Noah could stop her, she was standing outside.

"Sir, you ain't got no business with these good people here. I'm the one you lookin' for. It was me what ended Massa Ben's life. These folks just

took me in and fed me. Mr. Noah, I sure thank you and Miz Nelly . . . ."
She never saw the blow comin' that knocked her into the dirt.

Noah stood but the insistent pressure of Nelly's hand on his arm kept
him from going out of the door.

The younger Quint pulled Lovie to her feet and tied her hands behind
her back. Throwing her in the back of the buckboard that they had
brought with them the older Quint leaned forward, "Freeman, I'm gonna
let you live today, but I may not always be so generous. You owe me, boy,
and someday, someday soon you're gonna pay."

Dust swirled upward and momentarily obscured Noah's view of his sister's crumpled body in the bed of the vanishing wagon.

* * *

Three days passed before the buckboard again swung into the soft red
dirt, made a wide circle, and slowed down only long enough to heave the
broken, bloody body of a woman into the dust.

Noah came running from the barn, but by the time he got to the front
of the house the buckboard was bouncing back down the road. Squatting,
he lifted Lovie's bloody head. She spoke through broken teeth.

"Noah, I'm sure sorry to bring all this trouble to your doorstep. I ain't
wanted nothin' like this to happen."

"Sssh, don't talk, Lovie. You gonna be fine, and we gonna get through
this. Be a family, all of us."

"That a good dream all right. I would of sure liked that. Liked to see
those boys grow up to be big and strong. They enjoy some of this here freedom that everybody be talking 'bout. Nelly goin' to have that little gal she's
wantin'. I can tell, that baby be ridin' so high, that's how girls is. I sure wish
I could be here to see her, bound to be a pretty little thing."

"Lovie, I'm sorry. I wanted to stop them. How can I be free if I can't
even protect my family? They ain't gonna never let me or nobody like me
be free. It ain't right for somebody to just ride right up to my door and
drag folks out my house like I ain't no kind of man. It ain't right."

Struggling to raise her broken body from the dirt, Lovie laid her hand
on Noah's arm, "Don't you go feelin' bad. This ain't your shame. It belongs

to them what earned it. Can't nobody hold you responsible for the blackness in some other man's heart. Tell Sister Nelly I sure glad to make her acquaintance—and Noah. . . ."

Noah leaned down closer to hear the garbled words Lovie was struggling to force out. Stroking her forehead he tried to quiet her, "Please, Lovie don't . . . ."

"Got to say everything now. Ain't gonna be no time later. When my little niece is born, put a little piece of me on her. I sure liked being Lovie Free Lady. Pass that name on to her. The freedom gonna come to her, her children and grands and greats. That's where the freedom gonna come."

* * *

Two months later, on the first full moon after the birth of his daughter, Noah stood in a golden circle of the moonlight with his baby stretched skyward, "Lovie and the other ancestors, I present to you the next step in our journey, Lovie Free Lady Freeman. She's gonna carry us to the next stop on the freedom ride. She goin' places ain't none of us never dreamed, and we all goin' be so proud. Lovie, dear sister, I miss you every day, and every time I look at my sweet baby I think of you."

At that moment the baby girl opened her green eyes wide and smiled at her daddy. Noah was so full of love that he never noticed the horse and rider sitting in the darkness, just beyond the circle of light.

Chapter Five

by James Reasoner

Almost two decades had passed since the U.S. Army had established a camp on the bluff overlooking the Trinity River and named it after General William Jenkins Worth, one of the heroes of the recently concluded Mexican War. The camp had become a fort, and over the years a town had grown up around the military post and taken the same name— Fort Worth.

It was a busy place. Following the end of the Late Unpleasantness, ranchers in South Texas had started driving their cattle north to the railheads in Kansas. One of the main trails followed by those dust-choked pilgrimages went right through Fort Worth, and the herders often stopped here for a few days, letting the stock graze on the fine grass that grew alongside the twisting branches of the Trinity before pushing on to the Red River and Indian Territory beyond.

That meant the cowboys who drove that stock got to rest up for a few days, too, and that involved paying visits to some of the numerous saloons, dance halls, gambling dens, and houses of ill repute that sprang up to service their needs.

And that meant there was never any shortage of willing "sheep" to be shorn by John Howard Malone.

Since he didn't sleep much these days, he nearly always had a game going on in one of the saloons, night and day. Strong, slender fingers that had once gripped a cavalry officer's saber now caressed the pasteboards instead, sending them flicking out around the table with practiced ease. Gray-blue eyes that had narrowed in anticipation as Malone led his men into battle now intently watched the faces of the other players, and the strategic sense that had allowed Malone's company of raiders to emerge victorious in most of their battles enabled him to rake in many more pots than he lost. The stakes weren't life and death anymore, of course, as they had been during the war, but he still got some pleasure from winning. And of course, every hand he won meant that much more money to buy whiskey, and that much more whiskey helped deaden the pain and lay to rest the nightmares that haunted his restless slumber nearly every time he was foolish enough to try to sleep.

"Take two," said the big cowboy who sat across the table from Malone in the current game as he pitched a couple of cards on the stack. Malone dealt the replacements and saw the split-second flash of pleasure in the man's eyes, there and gone like the distant flicker of heat lightning. The fella had hoped for something, and gotten it.

Malone's impassive face didn't reveal what he had just learned. His tanned features were as still and calm beneath his moustache as the surface of a lake on a windless day. Nothing moved but his eyes as he studied his own cards. He didn't have much—a pair of fives, a jack, a three, a two. When the draw came around to him, he threw away the three and the two and dropped two cards from the deck in front of him.

Well, what do you know about that, he thought as he picked them up and added them to his hand. A jack—and another jack. A full house. Good enough to win most hands.

He wasn't sure about this one.

The cowboy sitting across from him had something good; Malone knew that. Whether or not it would beat a full house was up to chance, so Malone had to decide whether to trust his luck. Truth be told, it hadn't let him down all that many times.

Marie had been one of those times.

Surely it was just bad luck that had led him to fall in love with and marry a hot-blooded woman like Marie Duquesne, a woman who had been unable to remain faithful to her husband while he was off fighting in the war. Especially when Nate Sinclair, a handsome young man who was wealthy enough to pay somebody to go in his place, had started paying a mite too much attention to her. And what else could it have been except pure bad luck that had put Sinclair in Marie's bed on the very day that her loving husband returned home from the war, so that he walked in on them while they were in the middle of—

Malone's fingers tightened on the cards. With his other hand he shoved some coins into the center of the table to raise the bet.

Before that terrible day in Ohio, back in the summer of '65, good fortune had smiled on him pretty often. He had lived through the war, hadn't he? That was more than a lot of men could say. And his cavalry raiders had been involved in some pretty fierce scrapes there in Louisiana during the last couple of years of fighting.

It was good luck—and an empty belly—that had brought a hungry runaway slave into the company's camp one night. Malone had taken an instant liking to the husky young man called Noah, who clearly had a lot of natural intelligence despite his lack of education. There was an old black man with him who introduced himself as Preacher John. The old pelican liked to talk, and he'd explained to Malone that he and the boy were on their way to Texas.

That was all well and good, but Malone had need of a couple of good scouts. Noah and Preacher John didn't know the Louisiana countryside any better than Malone and the rest of the Yankee cavalrymen did, but they could move around easier without being noticed and they could talk to the slaves who still remained on the plantations. They ran the risk of being taken for runaway slaves—and Noah, of course, actually fit that description—but they were willing to take that chance after Malone fed and befriended them.

As it turned out, Preacher John could read a little, and he'd been trying to teach Noah. Malone helped out with that project, and Noah took to it like a hog to molasses. That helped an unlikely friendship spring up between the runaway slave and the Yankee cavalry captain from Ohio. Noah was willing to postpone his journey to Texas in order to stay and help Malone, and Preacher John had remained with the company, too.

In the Fort Worth saloon, the bet went around the table a couple of times, with some of the players raising and others dropping out, until the only ones left in the hand were Malone and the big cowboy. The cowboy was still trying to let on like he didn't have much in the way of cards, but Malone knew better. The cowboy raised. Not too much, not enough to tip his hand, but enough to goose the pot pretty good. Malone considered betting it all, thinking that might cause the cowboy to fold. But he couldn't be sure that his full house was going to beat whatever hand the cowboy held.

He thought about Marie, and knew that no man's luck ran to the good all the time.

But it sure had been good that day when Malone's raiders had run smack-dab into a bunch of Rebel cavalry and got mixed up in a fierce running battle where the advantage swung first one way, then the other, then back again. Malone had found himself engaging three of the Rebs. His pistol was empty, but so were the guns they carried. They hacked at him with their sabers instead, and it was all he could do to hold them off. He had already gotten cut a couple of times and knew that eventually they would overwhelm him and chop him to pieces.

So he had gone a little crazy, he supposed, and swung his saber so fast that it was almost blinding the way the sun flickered off the blade, and he spurred his horse so that it rammed against one of the Confederate mounts and knocked a way clear, and then Malone was galloping out of that trap for all he was worth. Would have made it, too, if his horse hadn't stumbled and gone down.

The Rebels were right behind him, of course, and would have ridden him down if Noah hadn't dashed out of the woods alongside the road, where he and Preacher John had been watching the battle anxiously. Noah had grabbed Malone and dragged him out of the way of those thundering hooves, and then as the last of the Rebel cavalrymen had raced past, damned if Noah hadn't jumped up and tackled that son of a gun, knocking him right out of the saddle.

Malone caught his breath as fast as he could, snatched up his saber from where he'd dropped it in the road, and jumped on that Rebel's horse. Noah had already knocked the man out with a couple of powerful blows.

The tables had turned. Malone went after the Rebels, instead of the other way around. When he caught up to them, the odds were still two to one, but he knew he would win. Fate had interceded on his behalf, in the person of Noah, and Malone's confidence was back.

He had cut those Rebels right down, like wheat in a field.

After that the bond between Noah and Malone was stronger than ever. Noah had saved his life, and Malone would never forget that.

They didn't say goodbye until the war was over. Noah and Preacher John headed on west to Texas, where it was Noah's dream to have a farm or a ranch of his own. Malone went back home to Ohio, to the loving wife he thought was waiting for him.

What he'd found there had made him doubt his luck for a long time. He wasn't sure even now if he would ever fully believe in it—or in much of anything else—ever again.

But he did believe he could win this poker hand, he decided. He raised right back at the cowboy. Not everything he had on the table, but enough to make the man scowl and hesitate.

Not for long, though. With an almost violent motion, the cowboy pushed in enough coins to meet the bet and said, "Call!"

"Full house," Malone said as he placed his cards face up on the table. "Jacks and fives."

The cowboy slapped his hand down. Malone saw the spades—five of them. A flush was a mighty good hand, all right. But it didn't beat Malone's full house.

He reached for the pot.

"Wait just a damned minute."

Malone paused with his hands hovering over the welter of coins and crumpled bills in the middle of the table. His eyes narrowed as he looked at the cowboy. "Why should I wait?" he asked. "I won that hand fair and square."

"I ain't so sure about that."

Malone halfway expected that blustery answer. And as he sighed, he knew he had to do something about it.

"Are you saying that I cheated?"

"I'm just wonderin' if that third jack came out of your sleeve, mister. I've heard about you Fort Worth slickers."

Malone tried to control his temper as he said, "In the first place, I'm not from Fort Worth. In the second, you can ask anybody in here if I deal an honest game. Most of them know me and know that I do." He eased back in his chair, withdrawing his arms and leaving the pot where it was. "In the third place, I don't like being accused of something that I didn't do. I'll thank you to apologize, sir. Considering the fact that you've been drinking quite a bit, I'm willing to write off your insulting comment as being due to the whiskey, and I'll accept your apology and we'll say no more about this."

Malone had hoped to overwhelm the man with words, but he saw right away that it wasn't going to work. The cowboy was too drunk, and his pride had been stung too badly by the defeat. He said, "In the first place, you're a damn cheatin' tinhorn, and in the second, forget it—"

The obscenity was drowned out by the scrape of the chair legs as he surged to his feet and reached for the butt of the revolver holstered at his waist.

Malone came up even faster. His left hand shot out as he leaned across the table. The fingers clamped around the wrist of the cowboy's gun hand as the Colt cleared leather. The explosion of the shot was deafening in the saloon's low-ceilinged confines. The bullet blasted down into the table, tearing the green cloth, chewing splinters from the wood beneath, and scattering the pot. Malone's right fist came around and crashed into the cowboy's jaw. The cowboy's head skewed to the side from the force of the blow. His gun slipped from his fingers and thudded to the table as his knees unhinged. Malone let go of his wrist and let him fall. The cowboy toppled to the floor, banging his chin hard on the edge of the table as he went down.

Malone took a deep breath. His pulse raced and pounded inside his head. He looked at the bullet-damaged table and realized that could have been him. He had seen too much fighting during the war—and since—to get queasy when he realized just how close to death he had come, but his jaw still clamped tightly for a moment.

The jingle of spurs made him look up. Four grim-faced cowboys were approaching the table. Friends of the man he had just knocked out, Malone supposed, and he wondered if he was going to have to fight them, too.

The oldest of the men, who had a weathered face and the squinting eyes of a man who lived his life outdoors, stepped forward as his three companions stopped. He nodded to Malone and said, "Name's Deke Farrell. Trail boss o' the outfit that boy's ridin' with." Farrell's hand gestured toward the unconscious man on the floor. "I'm much obliged to you for not killin' him, mister. We was watchin' from the bar, and you'd have been within your rights to put a bullet in him. Hank can be a fractious son of a gun, but he's a good hand when he ain't been guzzlin' too much fire-water. We'll just take him on back to the outfit's camp, if that's all right with you."

Malone nodded. "Fine with me. You might want to keep him there until he gets over being angry."

"Oh, he won't get over it. Not Hank. But we'll be pullin' out 'fore dawn tomorrow, so he won't have a chance to come lookin' for you. Better keep an eye out for him in a couple o' months, though, after we've delivered the herd and the boys are all on their way back home. He might try to look you up then."

Malone nodded again and said, "Thanks for the advice." He didn't add that he might not be in Fort Worth by that time. He avoided trouble as much as he could. That tended to be the smart thing to do.

Besides, he didn't want to be forced to kill anybody again. He had done enough of that during the war—and after . . .

Ah, Marie.

* * *

For a word with only four letters in it—three, actually, since one of them was repeated—"free" sure was mighty big. It was part of the name Noah had taken for himself after the war, so everybody would know what he was. Noah Freeman, he called himself. Freeman. Free man. Lord, it still sounded good, even after a few years.

It was part of his daughter's name, too; twice, in fact. Lovie Free Lady Freeman, she was called, after the sister that Noah had lost track of for years and then found again so briefly before tragedy had stolen her away. Some people might think the name was a mite too much, but to Noah's way of thinking a colored person couldn't use the word "free" too many times. No, sir.

Why, he had even called the ranch he'd started here in Central Texas "Free Land." That name was like a burr under the saddle to some folks around here, especially the owner of the neighboring ranch, Bear Coltrain, who had his eye on Noah's spread. And Sheriff Quint Carpenter didn't like it, either. It reminded him too much of his days as a slave catcher, back during the war and before, and how out of all the runaway slaves he'd been sent after, the only one who had ever gotten away clean was Noah. Who would have thought that Quint would wind up packing a badge here in the same parts as Noah's ranch? Fate took some funny turns.

But Noah had a feeling fortune was going to smile on him from here on out. He had a beautiful, loving wife, a couple of fine young sons, and now a baby daughter who was growing like a weed. Already Lovie was toddling around the place and jabbering fit to beat the band.

The boys could read a little. Noah had seen to that. And when the time came, Lovie would learn, too. Folks had to be able to read to get along good in the world. Noah firmly believed that. He had learned it from Preacher John, and from Cap'n Malone.

He missed Preacher John, he thought as he rode across his range, checking on the small but growing herd he had put together. The old man was over in East Texas somewhere, doing the Lord's work. As for the Cap'n . . . well, Noah hadn't seen him much since the war ended, but he often wondered what had happened to the officer after he helped Noah buy his land and then disappeared. Noah knew that white men who treated blacks like equals were rare. After falling in with the Yankees the first time, across the river from Vicksburg, Noah had learned mighty quick that for all their high-flown words about freeing the slaves, the northerners were just as likely as anybody else to hate colored folks. Maybe more so. When it came to coloreds, Noah had heard it said that southerners hated the race but loved the individuals, while northerners loved the race but hated the individuals. Lots of truth in that, he thought.

But not in Cap'n Malone's case. He didn't care one way or the other about the color of a man's skin. He took everybody as they were and judged them by how they acted.

Noah stiffened in the saddle and reined his horse to a stop as he saw three men ride out of a thicket of post oaks and lope their horses toward him. He didn't recognize them right off, but they came from the direction of Bear Coltrain's ranch. Neither Noah nor Bear actually owned all the range where they grazed their herds, which led to occasional disputes over which cattle had the right to be where. And Coltrain was the sort of man who just naturally liked to push against any boundaries. The men who rode for him followed his lead.

Noah thought about turning his horse around and riding away from here as quick as he could. But that would be running, and he'd done plenty of that in his life. More than enough, starting way back there at Massa Ellerbee's plantation.

As that memory went through his head, Noah leaned over and spat on the ground. He didn't call any man "massa" anymore, but there was no way to change the past. All he could do was disdain it.

As the three riders came closer, they began to look familiar to Noah. Coltrain riders, all right. He glanced down at the stock of the Henry rifle that rode in a saddle sheath under his left leg. He wanted to pull the weapon out, but such a hostile move might just start trouble that could be avoided.

The Coltrain hands brought their mounts to a stop about twenty feet from Noah. One of them thumbed back his battered, sweat-stained hat and said, "What are you doin' over here, nigger? This is Bear Coltrain's range."

"Probably lookin' to steal some o' Mr. Coltrain's stock," one of the other cowboys put in.

"I don't steal nothin' from nobody," Noah declared. "And this is my range. I been runnin' my cows on it ever since I started Free Land."

"Well, it's Coltrain's now. He's movin' part of his herd on it next week. So you got till then to get your scrawny beeves off it. Bear sent us over to your place to give you the news, but meetin' up with you like this saves us part of the ride, I guess."

Noah struggled to control the anger and the fear he felt. "He can't do that. It ain't right. When a man's been usin' part of the range, another man can't just come along and tell him to get off."

"That might be true if he was white. Custom like that don't apply to niggers."

Noah opened his mouth, about to say that he would go to the law about this, but then he realized that the law in these parts was Sheriff Quint Carpenter and his equally brutal son and deputy, Quint Two. There had been another Carpenter boy, Ben, who had also served as one of his father's deputies, but Noah's sister Lovie had been forced to kill him when he continued to abuse her.

No, Noah couldn't look to the law for help.

But if he could find some of the other ranchers in the area who sympathized with him, he might be able to put some pressure on Coltrain to honor the customs of the region. Coltrain wasn't well liked in general. He was a Yankee, after all, one of the legion of carpetbaggers who had swarmed into Texas after the war and taken over. He couldn't get away with this. He just couldn't.

The spokesman for the three cowboys facing Noah squinted at him and said, "You know, I don't like the look in your eye, boy. I think you're gonna be one o' them uppity niggers who don't do what he's told. Maybe we'd best show you how things are gonna be around here from now on."

Noah's hand twitched. He wanted so bad to reach for the Henry. But it was too late for that now. The three men all wore handguns. Before he could haul the rifle out of its sheath, they would draw those sixes and fire, and they'd blow him right out of the saddle.

But the horse under him was a good one, a rangy lineback dun, so Noah did the only thing he could.

With a yell, he whirled the dun around and kicked it into a gallop. If he could get back to his sturdily-constructed ranch house before they caught him, he could stand them off. He was sure of it.

A startled, angry yell came from behind him. "Get him! Get that nigger!"

Hooves pounded. Noah raced across the range with the three cowboys in pursuit. At first he thought the dun was going to be able to outrun their mounts. He actually pulled away from them, increasing his lead a little.

But then the dun faltered, and the cowboys whooped in anticipation as their horses thundered on. Noah glanced over his shoulder, disregarding the old axiom that said never to look back because something might be gaining on you. He saw the lariat sailing through the air toward him, cast in a wide loop . . .

Then it settled over him and was jerked tight around his chest so that he couldn't breathe or yell or do much of anything as he was pulled out of the saddle. He slammed hard into the ground and that knocked even more air out of his lungs. He lay there, his mouth opening and closing like that of an old catfish freshly pulled out of a creek, as Coltrain's men dismounted and surrounded him. He knew they were going to give him a thrashing and he wanted to fight back, but there was nothing he could do.

Not for the first time in his life, a booted foot thudded savagely into his ribs. The impact rolled him over onto his belly. He huddled there, absorbing a couple of more kicks.

Pain drove away the futility he had felt gripping him. Too much, he thought as his fingers clawed at the rope around his chest. He had taken too much in his life, allowing men like these to do whatever they wanted to him. Either that, or he had run away.

But no more. He got his fingers under the lariat and pushed himself up with his legs, pulling the rope up and off of him as he came to his feet. That took the cowboys by surprise, so that all they could do for a second was stare at him. Clearly, they hadn't expected a colored man to put up a fight.

Noah seized the moment and slashed the rope across the face of one of the men. He cried out in pain. Noah continued turning and swung a fist at the second man, connecting solidly and knocking the cowboy back a couple of steps. Using his momentum to pivot his body even more, Noah lowered his head and bulled straight ahead into the third man. He let out a furious shout as they crashed together and the cowboy went over backward. Noah was almost blinded by rage now, and all he wanted to do was get his hands around his enemy's throat and choke the life out of him.

He might have done it, too, if the man he had slashed with the rope hadn't recovered his wits enough to yank the iron at his hip out of leather and spring forward. Noah never saw the gun rise and fall, but he sure enough felt it smash against the back of his head. Every muscle in his body went limp, and the red haze of anger that had tinted his vision was replaced suddenly by an encroaching tide of darkness.

"You damn stupid nigger! You done made things a lot worse for yourself. You're gonna pay for what you just did!"

Those shouted words were the last thing Noah was aware of before oblivion claimed him.

* * *

The man on horseback who had been watching the confrontation from deep in the post oak thicket smiled as he saw Noah Freeman being pistol-whipped. Noah was going to be mighty busy for a while, getting the beating of his life from Coltrain's boys. The watcher just hoped that they wouldn't stomp the uppity nigger all the way dead.

He wanted Noah alive, so that he could fully appreciate what was going to happen next—and suffer from it.

Clucking to his horse, the watcher turned and rode toward Free Land, where that pretty little wife of Noah's was about to have some unwanted company.

* * *

Dead men shouldn't be able to feel any pain, so Noah reckoned he had to be alive.

Because he hurt like blazes. Lord, he hurt.

After a while, he pushed himself onto hands and knees and then staggered to his feet. He would have fallen again if the dun hadn't been standing close enough so that he could reach out and grab hold of a stirrup. He stumbled closer and leaned against the horse's side. That made the dun a little nervous, but it didn't bolt. Noah was grateful for that.

In fact, he was grateful just to be alive. Fighting back against white men like that had indeed been a damned stupid thing to do, as one of them had pointed out just before they whaled the tar out of Noah.

But it had felt so good to smash his fist into the face of one of them and to slash the other one with the rope. To strike a blow after all these years, after all the blows that had fallen on him.

Maybe it was worth getting the tar whaled out of him.

After a while he felt strong enough to climb up into the saddle. He pointed the dun toward home.

Nelly was going to raise holy ned when she saw him. He knew that both eyes were swollen almost shut, and every time he tried to move the muscles of his face he felt the pull of dried blood. He must look like something out of a nightmare. When he looked down at himself he didn't see much blood on his clothes, but from the feel of his body he was covered already with angry bruises. Once he stiffened up, he wouldn't hardly be able to move for a few days.

But he would have to force himself, because he had to try to rally some support against Bear Coltrain's range-hog tactics. The Texans might not be too eager to help a colored man, but if he pointed out that Coltrain might try to grab some of their range next, that might make a difference.

Every step the dun took sent fresh jolts of pain through Noah's battered body. He felt better when he came in sight of the ranch house, though. But he was a little puzzled when the boys didn't run out to meet him, as they usually did when he came home.

Something prickled along his backbone. Something cold and scary.

Noah pushed the dun into a faster walk.

When he reached the house, he still hadn't seen anyone. He dismounted clumsily because of his already-stiffening muscles and let the reins drop to the ground. The dun wouldn't wander off. Stepping into the doorway, he said, "Nelly? Nelly, you in here? Boys . . ."

He stopped as he heard a sob.

His eyes needed a moment to adjust to the dimness inside the house after the bright sunshine outside. Then his anxious gaze found Nelly sitting at the table, her shoulders slumped, her hands over her face as she cried. Noah Jr. stood on one side of her, Jessup on the other, trying unsuccessfully to comfort her. Noah forgot all about his own aches and pains as he saw how upset his wife was, and newfound rage welled up inside him as he noted that the dress she wore had been ripped and torn so that she was barely able to pull it back around her and cover herself.

"Nelly!" he cried out as he rushed to her side. The boys stepped back as Noah took hold of her arms and lifted her to her feet. "Nelly, what happened to you?"

Red-rimmed eyes stared wildly at him as if she didn't recognize him right off. But then she clutched at him and said, "Noah! Oh, Noah! It . . . it was that deputy . . . the one they call Quint Two . . . He . . . he rode up and forced his way into the house . . ."

Noah's hands tightened on her arms without him even being aware of it. "What did he do?" The words grated out of Noah's mouth. "What did he do to you?"

"That . . . that don't matter . . . I don't care about that."

Noah was about to tell her that he cared, when Nelly said something else that struck him dumb and made cold horror wash through him.

"It's the baby!" she said, and Noah realized now that he hadn't seen Lovie when he came in. "Oh, God, Noah . . . He took the baby!"

Chapter Six

by Mary Rogers

The bright green wagon with ruby-colored wheels swayed and creaked as the sweating team of gray mules hauled it up the dusty rise. Once the wagon had belonged to an apple peddler who'd made his way from Missouri to Texas selling the fruit to housewives, children, and shopkeepers who took the apples as fast as the peddler could take their money. When the cargo was gone, the peddler sold the team and wagon to a Fort Worth merchant and hired on as a drover pushing cattle north. The merchant kept the wagon a for a year and then let Duff McNamara have it, the team and the tack for $100, a price that emptied Duff's pockets, but he paid his money and fretted only a little about how he'd buy his dinner that night.

The very next morning he learned that a young woman had arrived in Fort Worth looking for someone to haul some freight to Fort Concho in West Texas, and Duff thought of this not as a lucky turn of events but as the very hand of God making all the crooked ways straight for him. Hadn't he been dreaming of going out to the frontier's western edge before the world caught up with it? Hadn't he been praying he'd find a way to make his beautiful wagon profitable?

Mary Mills had agreed to pay Duff the princely sum of $50 to deliver her, a heavy bedstead, a five-drawer chest, her grandmother's rocking chair, a tall case clock, and a small barrel of bone china to her sister's adobe house near Fort Concho. Duff had agreed quickly, only a little sorry that there was no time to paint the name of his photographic business on the side on the wagon before they pulled out of town.

In fact, Duff McNamara had been a photographer of some renown in St. Louis, but he'd grown tired of taking portraits of wealthy German immigrants and fancied keeping the photographic record of the frontier while Indians still roamed the plains. He made his way to Texas, planning to photograph government forts that were being built as a line of defense against the Comanche, Kiowa, and the Apache.

He thought Fort Worth would be a rugged foothold on the western edge of civilization, but he was disappointed. By the time Duff rolled into town in the spring of 1869 the soldiers had been gone for years, replaced by a rough-and-tumble town that offered cowhands trailing herds north all the diversion they could want—and the town's four church congregations all the sins they could pray over.

Still, Duff set about keeping a photographic record of what he witnessed. He asked a teen-aged boy who trailed after one big herd, tending to the remuda, to pose for a photo. He took another picture of the cook with his chuck wagon as he prepared to ford the river at Daggett's Crossing just below the bluff where the town perched. Late that afternoon Duff rode into the cowboy camp and asked to take a few more pictures. He liked the Mexican drovers who wore wilted roses in their hatbands. They'd discovered the roses growing on a fence surrounding a house that squatted beside the trail. The woman living in the house had smiled and nodded permission when they asked for the flowers. But the Mexicans had been shy about standing before the camera while the other cowboys watched. They laughed and pushed each other, said things in Spanish that Duff could not understand. One mounted his horse and rode away while the others hooted. In the end Duff had ridden out of that camp without his photo.

He took portraits of some of Fort Worth's leading citizens and climbed onto a second-story roof to capture an image of the town square filled with wagons. He made a little money, but he itched to find the real frontier. Now at last he was on his way.

Mary Mills sat on the high rough seat next to him, sweating in the hot morning sun. She patted her thin face with a red handkerchief and sighed. "Mr. McNamara, my sister must have lost her faculties. The commander at Fort Concho is so afraid for her that he sent two soldiers to escort her into the fort for safety's sake. She went, but in her last letter she said she does not plan to tarry. Why on earth would she want to stay in Indian country when she could be in Louisiana out of harm's way? Sometimes I think she is a fool. "

Duff McNamara, owner of the green apple wagon-turned-freight car and photographer's studio, clutched a pipe in his teeth although there was no fire in the bowl. He took the pipe from his mouth and smoothed his dark beard with the back of his hand. He held the reins lightly.

"Maybe she has no interest in safety, miss. Didn't you say her husband was pushing a herd north? Could be your sister wants to be where he left her when he returns."

Mary looked sideways at the man beside her. He was in his mid-twenties, she guessed, about her age, a nice enough looking fellow with pink cheeks and dark curls that twisted from beneath the high-crowned hat he wore. Its wide flat brim was good protection from the blistering sun, but she did not admire this ten-gallon headgear. She sniffed.

"Not north, Mr. McNamara. Everyone goes north. He's taking the herd to California! I wouldn't be surprised if he never returned," she said. Mary looked ahead at the rolling prairie. The tall grass was brittle and curling in the summer heat and the ruby wheels spun little rivulets of dust over the iron rims.

Duff let her remarks pass. He was focused on a line of pecan trees a quarter mile ahead. "There's a creek there," he said nodding in the direction of the trees. "We'll water the mules and have a bite of bread and cheese."

Mary watched three buzzards circle high above the trees.

"Texas pallbearers," Duff remarked, but Mary said nothing, and the wagon rattled into the shady oasis. A hot wind toyed with the filthy hem of her dark cotton skirt and tugged at the wide brim of her straw hat, but she put up a slender hand and caught it before it went cartwheeling away.

"What's that?" she said, suddenly alert, straining to hear.

"What?"

"I heard something."

Duff picked up the rifle braced against the wagon seat and listened. The hot wind stirred the green canopy above their heads, and shadows played across the creek's muddy water.

"Only the wind, miss—only this devil's wind blowing right up from hell," he said, but he did not relax. He'd heard all the stories about the ferocious Comanche war parties that roamed the plains. He longed to take a warrior's photograph, but now the hair on the back of his neck stood up, and he prayed that savages did not hide in the undergrowth ready to snatch his scalp and his mules.

Mary yanked on his sleeve. "Shhhh." He stood still, listening, rifle in hand, knees flexed, ready to jump down from the wagon or fire if something stirred. There it was again, the faintest whimper, not like wind at all. This time Duff heard it too.

Mary spotted the bundle first, a dirty package of rags beneath a tree. She climbed down from the wagon's high seat and cautiously approached the package. It moved. Then a tiny fist waved from between the folds.

"It's a baby! Mr. McNamara, it's a baby!" she shouted.

Duff hurried over to look down at the bundle in Mary's hands. "God A'Mighty, it's a colored child." They both looked about, expecting to see the babe's mother, but they saw only hoof prints in the sand. "What are we to do with this?" Duff asked, and then he knew exactly what to do. Duff hurried back to the wagon to retrieve his tripod and camera equipment.

* * *

Earlier, Noah had roared and bolted out the door determined to rescue his child. The kidnapper waited knowing Noah would come for Lovie.

That beating was more brutal than the last, but somehow Noah survived that and a bungled attempt at hanging only to find it was just the beginning of his sorrows.

For more than a day Noah lay in a coma, and the old woman who hovered over him thought he was deciding whether to stay in this world or follow his sweet Nelly into the next. She bound up his wounds, but she wondered if he could return to them whole.

"Looky here, Mama. He comin' round."

"Let me see, chile. Oh yes. Oh yes. You with us once more, Mr. Noah Freeman. We thought you gone for good, but here you be, coming back from some dark place to see the Lord's good day."

The voice was a balm, thick and cool, and Noah swam through the gloom toward the voice. Waves of light sparkled and undulated above him, but he was a dreamer trapped at the bottom of a dark well. He saw flashes of fire but smelled no smoke. He heard the horses nicker. Cruel laughter rolled like thunder across his scorched brain. A rope snapped tight against his neck. He kicked the air, strangling, understanding then that night riders in white robes had expected him to come for his child. They'd let his wife and boys live so he could hear the news of his kidnapped daughter before they fell on him. He was trapped. The world splintered into a thousand bloody stars, and he was falling, falling, falling with no place to land.

Noah pushed toward the light, eager to breathe again. His head rolled to and fro and seemed to have a life of its own. He heard the cornhusks' dry rattle beneath him. He tried to open his eyes, tried to speak, but he wasn't strong enough to lift his heavy eyelids and his throat seemed filled with dust. He cried out as a dreamer cries in mumbled sobs and half-formed words. He pushed harder toward the surface.

A hand, hot and dry, touched his forehead, and Noah jumped. "It's alright, baby. Don't you fret. You right here with Mama Lou now. You safe and sound." He gulped in the cabin's thick air. He was almost home, almost there. He could feel the light, warm and yellow, covering him like a blanket.

The big woman bathed his face with a damp cloth and clucked encouragement. Noah heard the scrape of shoes on the dirt floor and knew someone stood close to the woman.

"He comin' round?" the man asked.

"Oh yes. Mr. Noah Freeman comin' back to us."

"What we gonna tell him?"

"Hush now," the woman hissed, but the man did not hush.

"How we gonna say Nelly and the boys burnt up by the Klux riders, his little girl stolen and probably dead too, his house gone, pig cooked to death, cow run off? Mama, what we gonna say?"

The man's voice was a raspy whisper. Noah's head rolled back and forth. He breathed in the man's stale scent of tobacco and sweat. His hand jerked up to the rope burns on his neck. His legs twitched. He moaned, but Mama Lou continued to bath his face. Her voice was thick as sorghum, almost a whisper.

"We gonna say the truth. That's all we can say. Klux riders tried to snatch his life like one of them snatched his baby girl. They got one, but not the other. Nelly and the boys gone now. He a strong young man. He alive so he have to live, and that's God's own truth too," she said,

Suddenly Noah opened his eyes for the first time in a full day. He blinked but made no sound. Mama Lou wiped away his tears. "Oh baby," she said. "I know. I know."

* * *

It took months for Noah to heal, but even after he could work in Mama Lou's garden or feed the pigs and chickens she and Uncle Daniel kept, his spirit continued to bleed. Noah believed that his very life was seeping away. He picked at his food. He never smiled and forgot entirely how to laugh. Each evening he limped around the pile of ashes that had been his home. When Mama Lou tried to talk with him, he stared out at the horizon and she worried that he was leaving them, slipping away like a little boat lost in the fog of some great dark river.

"Noah, we need you here," she told him one evening. "You have a strong mind. You can read. You brave enough to vote in last year's election. Not all these po' ol' colored men do that. Some still have the slave's mind, still trying to do fo' massa. You marched yo' fine self right between the lines of soldiers guarding the votin' box and looky here what come of it. Now the great state of Texas gots nine black men helping write the new constitution. We gonna have black senators and congressmen in Austin too. You watch. Wouldn't be so, if not for strong men such as yourself. Noah, you and your kind the future and the hope of all the colored peoples."

Noah turned his green eyes on Mama Lou then, remembering that election in 1868. Federal troops sent to maintain order and see that voting went smoothly camped below the bluff north of the courthouse, and members of the Union League rode through the countryside coaxing former slaves to the vote. They met with more resistance than in other places, but on election day a few black men gathered on the square, eyeing the double line of soldiers that stood outside the courthouse polling place.

Some of the soldiers in the line were black too, and that gave the would-be voters courage. A few white men passed between the Federal guards, their cheeks flushed, their eyes focused straight ahead. The soldiers, black and white, stood tall too. This was history's business, and they all knew it.

At last a Union Leaguer pushed one black man forward. The one-time slave took a few quick steps, hesitated, and looked back. The Union League man winked and nodded, and the former slave marched resolutely to the polls. Noah followed him, aware that the town's white leaders watched from a distance, their arms folded across their chests.

Only the wind spoke, a low moaning sound that rose up from the river and skated across the bluff to unfurl the American flag that stood beside the courthouse. Most of the white men who watched were Confederate veterans who refused to take the "Ironclad Oath," a declaration that they had never been disloyal to the government. Once respected leaders recognized not just in this little town but in the state's capital, now they were disenfranchised with no say in this new government. They watched the line of voters for a time and then went into their shops and began a furious cleaning of shelves and cupboards.

When Noah came out of the courthouse that day, he felt light and heavy at the same time. Voting, he knew, was a sign of strength, only a white man's right until that bright morning, but he saw the angry look of the white shopkeeper who swept the boardwalk in front of his business. Noah recognized hatred in the man's eyes. Already a group of young black men loitered on a sidewalk on the shady side of the street. An elderly white man wearing a bowler hat and a string tie tried to pass, but the one-time slaves would not yield any ground and the old man crossed the street rather than take them on. Noah knew there would be a price to pay for this day.

In less than a week word ran though the town that some blacks who had signed labor contracts refused to work. The Freedmen's Bureau, which had negotiated agreements between the one-time slaves and former slaveholders and heard complaints, was already on shaky ground and almost ready to shut its doors, leaving the frustrated parties to simmer in their own juices.

One of Judge Murdock's former slaves, then employed as a household domestic and nanny, boldly walked through the front door and sat down in the parlor, because a Union Leaguer had told her such was her right. It was the last straw for the judge who could hardly provide for his own children at the time. The former slave had lived in his house her entire life, but the judge had the woman's clothes and the furniture from her room set outside his fence.

"You may go and do as you like, since you no longer belong here," he told her.

Others in the dusty little town had the same sort of trouble. Captain Morgan's former slave had been retained as the cook, but the woman began arriving late each morning for work. One day the captain's frustrated wife beat the black woman with a willow switch. The former slave ran to the authorities and charged the captain's wife with assault and battery, and Captain Morgan was forced to pay a fine. Word traveled fast and laughter could be heard coming from the old slave shanties, but Noah thought it was not the last laugh.

Before the month was out, Noah heard that a group of men dressed in white robes had rallied in the town's square. They wore tall paper masks that covered their faces with little holes for their eyes.

"Miz Johnson say them Republicans and carpetbaggers best watch out," said Alice, Mama Lou's grandchild who worked in Martha Johnson's house.

"What you say, chile?" asked Mama Lou.

"That what I listen to Miz Johnson say to church ladies. They all say, 'Yes. Yes. You right there.'"

Noah knew blacks had better watch too. Some whites were chafing under the rules of Reconstruction, and they were angry that former slaves would have a say in shaping the new state constitution while they were kept from the polls because of their ties to the Confederacy. Reconstruction seemed more a punishment than a reorganization.

Noah had been proud of his stand that first election day, but he wondered if it hadn't made him more of a target for the night riders that whites called "The Klan" and blacks called "The Klux." Was that the reason he'd lost everything? Suddenly he felt some dark curtain in his mind part, and Noah knew Mama Lou spoke the truth. The old slave days were over, but streets in this new world were not paved with gold. They were free, but they hadn't yet reached the Promised Land.

Noah took her plump hands in his. "Mama, thank you for caring for me, but what I gonna do now? I miss my family. I'm filled with hate. I got no way to get back what I lost. My life not worth a tinker's damn."

"You wrong 'bout that, Noah Freeman. You so wrong about that," said Mama Lou. "You just started your ride."

* * *

The months slipped away like dark water beneath a bridge of time. Noah grew stronger, but he wore his grief like a heavy coat in a spring rain, and Mama Lou fretted over the state of his soul. He was pleasant, but he stood apart, alone and inconsolable.

One night Mama Lou persuaded Noah to attend a dance held in a small settlement of freemen a few miles south. At first he shook his head, but in the end she won the tug of war. By the time they arrived at the party a perfect circle of orange moon hung high in the inky sky, and loud talk and laughter filled the night. Everyone had brought something to eat and spread it on a rough table. A coal-oil lantern sat at each end of the table, but the moonlight was so bright the lanterns really weren't needed. Men, women, and children filled tin plates with beans and summer squash, fried rabbit, stewed squirrel, and cornbread. Uncle Daniel played a fiddle, and a light-skinned man thrummed a Jew's harp while another beat out a rhythm on a tub turned upside down. Jugs of corn liquor were passed among the men, and a few women filled pipes with tobacco and blew smoke into the cool air.

Alice asked him to dance. He shook his head. He watched the dancers as they twirled and hooted. He even smiled, but he was not ready to participate. Not yet. He stood in the shadows watching, but Alice kept circling back to him. "If you won't dance, come let Honey Banks tell you fortune," she coaxed.

"Don't believe in such nonsense," he said. Someone passed him a jug of corn whiskey, and Noah raised it to his shoulder. Since he'd lost Nelly and the boys, he'd developed a newfound taste for the homemade liquor. It seemed to soothe the fire inside him.

"She tell you somethin' good, I feels it. Come on let her tell you what tomorrow bring," said Alice.

"Go 'way, girl," said Noah, but after two more swigs from the jug, he let the girl lead him to the old woman.

"She come from long line of African queens and prophets," said Alice. Noah grunted his suspicion but followed her across the wide dirt yard that had been swept with a broom earlier that afternoon.

Honey Banks was the color of river sand, and Noah thought her eyes were as black as a witch's heart. When Alice asked if she'd tell Noah's fortune, Honey cocked her head to one side and studied the man for a long moment.

"Yes, little Alice, I will look into the future for this young man. Bring a lantern into my house there," she said pointing to a shanty at the far end of the row. She did not sound like the other blacks at the party. Her words were as crisp as a white man's Sunday collar. Noah thought she sounded more dignified than most of the whites he knew.

Alice ran to get one of the lanterns from the dining table and gave it to Noah. "You go on by yourself, now," said Alice and she pushed him toward the shack.

Noah stepped into the tiny room and found Honey lighting candles. A rough table stood in the center of the room; behind it was an armchair decorated with medallions of hammered bits of tin and bright glass beads. The chair seemed too large for this petite woman, but she turned gracefully to face him and perched lightly on this crude throne. Her hair was completely covered by a purple kerchief, and she wore no jewelry. Only her black eyes sparkled in the candlelight. Noah knew she was old, but she seemed somehow ageless.

She motioned for Noah to set the lantern on the table. She placed a basket on the other end of the table and laid a long knife beside it. He pulled another chair to the table and sat across from her.

"Let me have your hands," she commanded.

She stroked first one palm and then the other, pinched the fleshy pads of his fingers, bent close and studied the lines in his left hand and then his right. She leaned back resting her head against the curved back of the chair. She shut her eyes and began to hum.

"What is it? What you see?" asked Noah, the unbeliever.

Honey Banks rose slowly from her throne and opened the basket. She commanded him to hold the lantern higher so she could better see the contents. He did as she asked. Then she plunged her hand in and pulled out a wriggling snake as big around as her fist. In one fluid motion, she slammed the creature onto the table and cut off its head.

Noah jumped back, knocking over his chair as a fountain of blood spewed across his shirt.

"The blood tells all," said Honey. She reached into the basket again and retrieved a small animal skull. She chanted soft and low, words Noah could not understand, as she held the still-writhing reptile in the air and caught the blood in the skull. Noah stood transfixed by this spectacle, but she motioned for him to sit down again, and he obeyed.

She stirred the blood with one long, bony finger, then took Noah's hands again and painted a bloody X on the back of each and Noah saw that the nail on that single finger was long and thick. It scratched his skin. The action seemed to have cost her much energy, and she collapsed against the chair again with eyes closed.

"I see a long road for you, Mr. Noah Freeman, a good horse, a better friend and. . . ." her voice trailed away.

The music drifted through the open door. He could smell tobacco on the wind.

"And?" said Noah.

She closed her eyes and swayed back and forth like a candle flame caught in a draft. Her lips parted, and Noah could see her teeth blackened and rotting in the lantern light. Her foul breath reached across the table to him.

"I see a great wilderness marked by drought, thirsty riders in blue coats and Indian camps. I see sand and . . . ." She opened her eyes and leaned close to the blood-filled skull.

Honey Banks stirred the blood again and pointed the dripping finger at him. Crimson droplets splashed onto the table.

"I see. I see." She cocked her head; her glittering eyes fixed him to the spot. "Do not trade redemption for revenge, Noah Freeman," she said. Then she lifted the skull to her lips and drank.

Outside the music stopped, and Noah shot out of the chair. He saw her scarlet fingerprints on the white bone. As she looked straight at him, he stumbled backward, then turned and hurried into the yard.

Someone called out. "Look there. Trouble coming this way riding a pale horse—or two."

Everyone looked down the road. A group of men on horseback cantered toward them. Each rider wore a white robe that covered his horse's flanks. Each of their heads was covered with a tall white mask. Each carried a lighted torch, and the flames fluttered and flared in the breeze.

The black women shooed the children into the little shacks that had once been slave quarters. Teen-age girls took their places with the younger children. The men stepped in front of the women, who gave no ground as the riders came.

"You do the talkin'," one big man said to Uncle Daniel. "You the oldest man here and the best talker."

Uncle Daniel walked to the road. His hair was a white halo in the moonlight. "Gentlemen, they no cause for trouble here tonight," he said. "We have permission to be here. Mr. Tate Jones, owner of all this land and once the owner of some of these very people here, say we can gather here from time to time. He know we here tonight and don't mind we have a dance and a bite of supper together."

Uncle Daniel held himself tall and proud, but the nervous words had tumbled out like water rushing down a rainspout, exposing his anxiety. The riders' horses shied and stepped sideways. The torches cast an orange glow. No one spoke. "Can I help you?" Uncle Daniel said. Not a word was said. "What you men want?"

The riders looked down from their high perches, but no one answered the old man. The black men behind Daniel motioned for the women to move into the shacks. A few did, but most stayed put.

"We not doin' nothin' to cause you any worry," Daniel said. He waited, but still no one spoke. He could see the glittering blue eyes behind the mask of one and a milky eye behind another. The hair on his arms stood up.

"Well, then I bid you men a goodnight," he said and turned to walk away, but he had taken only two steps when he heard the whoosh of the lariat and felt the hard loop that dropped over his shoulders.

One of the women screamed.

"Hush up. We don't care about your dance," growled one of the riders.

"We're looking for a man calls himself Freeman. Give him to us, and you can go on with your party."

Uncle Daniel turned to face the riders. "No one named Freeman here, sir," he said.

The rope pinned Uncle Daniel's hands below his waist. The rider yanked the rope so hard the old man fell to his knees and then toppled over, landing face down in the dirt. "I'm asking one more time. We want a man calls hisself Freeman."

Noah knew that voice. It rumbled up from the depths of memory. It was Coltrain's voice. Noah was sure. He took a step, but a dark hand shot out and held him back. Startled Noah looked into the obsidian eyes of the man next to him. This stranger shook his head ever so slightly and another man stepped up close to Uncle Daniel. "Sir, there is no one here named Freeman," he said, looking up at the robed menace.

"No?" said the rider. "We'll see." Suddenly he began to pummel Uncle Daniel with a length of rope. The old man wriggled out of the loop and tried to cover his head with his hands. The other riders began to whoop and circle the shacks holding their torches high. The women shouted to their children to get out get out of the little houses and come to them.

Noah expected that at any moment one of the torches would be tossed onto a dry roof and the row of one-time slave shanties would become a bonfire, but just as quickly as they had come, the riders departed whooping and laughing as they went, holding the torches high in the bright moonlight, their glowing white robes flapping behind them.

Uncle Daniel touched his thick fingers to his scraped cheek, and Mama Lou blotted up the oozing blood. He stopped her busy hands. "They only want to scare us," he said. "No harm done. Let's dance."

A few frightened children whimpered, and their mothers held them close, cooing reassurances. The fiddler took up his bow again, but the party was over. From that moment on Noah knew he had to go, he just didn't know where or how.

* * *

Noah found Jake Pratt at his livery stable, as he knew he would. Jake was one of the few black men in town who had been a slave and now owned his own business. There were other livery stables, but Jake enjoyed the patronage of some of the town's most respected and prominent citizens. Never mind that such men could no longer vote and had no official say in how Texas would rise from its ruined past. They still wielded enormous power around the town square and beyond. Most were called "Captain" either as a measure of respect or because they had risen to that rank in the recent war that divided the country.

Jake had recently buried his wife, and he wore a black band on his bulging bicep as a show of mourning. He was drinking a cup of coffee when Noah sat down. Jake was old enough to be Noah's father, but the two had become friends, meeting first at a church baptism near Cold Springs. They had become occasional fishing companions, and now Noah needed this old friend's wise counsel.

Jake nodded a greeting but he waited for Noah to explain why he was there. He didn't have to wait long. Noah was not one for small talk. "Jake, the Klux after me and maybe all them that voted las' year. I got to leave this place, but where I goin'? How I live?"

Jake turned his round sweating face toward Noah. His dark eyes were alert, and his full lips curled into a half smile. He nodded. "Let me pray on that, boy," he said.

Jake looked at his shoes. He nodded again. After a time he stood up. "Come see me tomorrow, 'bout this time of day," said Jake. Noah sighed and walked away.

The next day Jake was saddling a lineback dun gelding when Noah walked into the stable. Jake looked up. "This for you, boy. You take this animal, and you ride right into that U.S. Army fort over to Jacksboro, and you enlist."

Noah jumped back as if he'd been shot. "I can't take this horse. I can't enlist."

"The government start letting colored folk join up some years back. Now what you say about the Klux mos' likely so. This a way out—the only way I can figure."

"But I can't pay for this horse," Noah protested.

"Others already pay some. I do some. Now this horse ready to go," said

Jake, pulling the cinch tight. He patted first one saddlebag and then the other, cataloguing its contents. "A change of clothes here. Hard tack and biscuits here," he said. "Coffee. Cartridges. Rifle. Blanket. No need to go any place but away from here, but don't you forget us," he said. The big man pressed a few coins into Noah's hand. "Neighbors took up a collection," he said.

Noah shook his head.

"You can't say no. It's done," said Jake. He held out a neatly folded piece of paper. "This says the horse is yours, bought and paid for. Can't have no army man think you a horse thief."

The two men faced each other. They embraced, and Jake pounded Noah's back as a sign of devotion and respect.

"You tell Mama Lou and Uncle Daniel where I goin'. You say my thanks," Noah said and then he swung into the saddle. "Tell them I love them."

Jake nodded.

* * *

For reasons he could not fully explain Noah didn't go to Fort Richardson at Jacksboro. Instead he turned west, then south, and a bit more than a week later found himself rolling out his blanket near a muddy river so narrow he could practically jump across it. On a flat plateau across the stream he could see the night guards at Fort Concho. He could hear music from the rowdy outpost called Saint Angela. He would have liked a bath and a hot meal, but he knew even in this remote corner of the frontier, citizens probably weren't too happy to see blue uniforms and perhaps even less enthusiastic about black faces.

He watched the stars pop out in a velvet sky and drifted into a restless sleep. Gunfire and shouts woke him. The moon was high, and he could see several drunken cowboys as they raced up and down the river on horseback, firing pistols in the air and shouting curses at the soldiers on the other side. The commotion lasted only a little while and then the cowboys staggered back into a saloon, bragging of their bravery.

The next day Noah rode across the shallow river and was stopped by the sentry. He told the man, who was also black, that he wanted to enlist. The guard eyed Noah's horse. "This unusual," he said.

Noah shrugged.

"Well, you may be lucky," the sentry said. "The post's not full just now, not since four men died of the runs, one of a fever and another got too much heat and sun to live."

The fort was hardly a complete compound, and Noah was surprised to see that soldiers both black and white worked beside civilian stone masons and carpenters to raise a row of officers' quarters and a long barracks. Just west of the fort, Noah could see that a stone building had almost been completed for the fort trader, and not too far from that a large frame house or hotel had already been finished.

Beside the hotel Noah could see a green wagon with red wheels. He'd seen wagons like that in Fort Worth, wagons loaded with Missouri apples. A man in a ten-gallon hat seemed to be painting a slogan on the side of the wagon. Noah watched the man for only a moment and then turned his attention to the matter of enlistment.

It was easier than he imagined. He went first to the officer of the day who asked a few questions about the horse. Noah showed him the bill of sale and the man shrugged.

"Well, the army always needs soldiers, " he said and sent Noah on to the post surgeon for a quick physical, then to the sergeant of the company. With the stroke of a pen Noah had become part of the 10th Cavalry, one of the buffalo soldiers who patrolled the great Texas frontier protecting settlers from raiding Indians, Mexican bandits, and other riffraff, but all that would come later.

That night there was trouble across the river in the sad little row of gray shacks where gamblers played faro and dance hall girls plied a more wicked trade. Noah heard gunshots and loud shouts.

"Always trouble there. Best stay clear of that place," one of the troopers advised.

Noah hoped he'd traveled so far trouble would never find him again. He crawled into his cot that night too tired to sleep, but he welcomed the memories of Nelly that came to him in the gloom. He saw her in sunlight with little Lovie in her arms and their son at her feet. He shook off thoughts of the ambush, the pain of recovery. He imagined Nelly's sweet smell, the warmth of her touch. He prayed that his baby girl was alive and safe somewhere and that one day he would meet her. He closed his eyes and would not think of the ashes in the wind.

Chapter Seven

by Mike Cochran / Mike Blackman

The news of Jake Pratt's death stunned Fort Worthers of all class and color. Everybody liked old man Pratt: He was a good man, a God-fearing man who would lend a fellow a horse till payday and who would pray for anyone afflicted with life's misfortunes. He treated his animals well, charged a fair price, and knew how to placate even the fussiest customers. More important, he knew his place. For a colored boy—they paid the ultimate compliment—Jake Pratt put some white people to shame, especially those rowdy cowboys who liked to shoot up the town on Saturday night, scaring children and chickens witless. Jake Pratt didn't cause a lick of trouble, and when you met him on the sidewalk he always gave you plenty of room and always tipped his hat. A tragedy, they said of his death: He seemed such a happy, fulfilled man.

"Self-inflicted suicide," the sheriff announced after he cut Jake down from the rafter. A local magistrate agreed.

Later, when a doctor inspected the body, he found one arm and both legs broken, and there appeared to be two small wounds, possibly bullet holes, barely discernible, at the base of Jake Pratt's skull.

"When a man's headstrong determined, he can do anything," the sheriff said. "Case closed."

* * *

Almost overnight everyone in Saint Angela knew about the baby. Mostly what people knew was that a few days earlier a white woman had arrived accompanied by a load of furniture, an odd little man with a big camera, and a baby that clearly wasn't hers. Or was it? One thing was clear: There wasn't a colored daddy in sight. Shameful, some said, her taking up with them types and birthing, no less! Where did she think she was? New York? Boston?

"Jus' like a Yankee," the talk went. "All nigger lovers."

New in town himself, Noah had not heard such talk when he and the lieutenant found the wounded trooper face-down in the street. By the time they dismounted, a man from the saloon had reached the trooper and cradled his head in his lap.

"Hold on, soldier, we're gonna make you all right," said the man who, by the light of the brilliant moon, Lieutenant Gibson recognized as a civilian worker at the fort, one of the Buck brothers. Doodad Buck.

"Private Freeman—get the doctor," the lieutenant ordered. "Now—skedaddle, double time!"

"Back of the saloon, second door," yelled Doodad who gingerly held the trooper's head, now bleeding steadily from a wound just over the right eyebrow. "Doc Tibbs should be there. Should still be sober!"

Noah ran as fast as his thick legs would carry him down the alley behind the saloon.

"Mr. Buck," Lieutenant Gibson asked, "what the Sam Hill happened—who shot this man?"

"Drunk cowboy best I could tell," said Doodad. "Was three of them. This one cowboy—he had a funny look to him, can't tell you directly why—he kept asking for more song singing and banjo playing. Said it made him think of his girl in Fort Worth. The trooper, he laughed at the cowboy and said he had to get back to the fort for guard duty."

The soldier lay still in Doodad's lap, not moving, not making a sound. The only sign of life was a thin rivulet of blood that oozed from his mouth.

The lieutenant put his ear to the trooper's chest.

"Where's the doctor?" Lieutenant Gibson screamed. He knew the trooper; it was Corporal Sims, one of his best soldiers, a career man with a fine wife and seven kids, who all looked just like their daddy, even the girls.

"I'm right here," someone shot back. "Out of the way, please."

Doc Tibbs, who this night reeked of only tobacco and perfumed body water, knelt beside the soldier. The lieutenant, Noah, Doodad, and a small crowd of onlookers gathered around. One held a lantern.

Doc suddenly stood and put away his stethoscope.

"You boys get this man to my office. Lay him on the table—careful!"

After the trooper was taken care of, Lieutenant Gibson asked Doodad and Noah to join him in the Cactus Saloon. They sat at a table near the far end of the long bar where a man in a jean-cloth shirt and scar across his nose was drinking.

"Anybody seen these boys before?" the lieutenant asked.

"No, not that I recall," said Doodad. "Just drunked-up strays."

Noah asked, "Who started the ruckus?"

"The one who shot the trooper," said Doodad, who for the first time noticed Noah's green eyes. "The crazy one."

"Crazy?" said Noah, looking at Doodad,

"Well, he began firing off his .45 into the ceiling ever' time the trooper started to put down his banjo. Nearly hit a girl coming out her room upstairs. He kept saying 'I'm looking for a new nigger in town. Banjo man, keep playin' and lemme see your eyes.'"

As Doodad spoke, the words apparently caught the attention of the man at the end of the bar; he was staring at Doodad, had put down his whiskey glass. Doodad went on, "The shooter got right in the banjo picker's face and said, 'Boy, I'm looking for a green-eyed nigger man, and you ain't it. You may thank your lucky stars. Play on, boy—play on your happy tunes.'" Doodad was looking at Noah when the man at the bar suddenly swung his head. Noah and the man's eyes locked. Noah tensed and wished he had his pistol. The man at the bar threw down the last of his drink, spun on a boot heel, and strode briskly toward the door.

Noah sat for a moment, unsure what to do, thinking where he might have seen the man before. He then excused himself and rushed for the saloon's swinging doors. Somebody was riding out of town. That's all he saw. Noah walked back to the table.

The lieutenant and Doodad were talking. "And nobody tried to stop it?"

"Nah," Doodad said, "some was fixin' to but they just asked him to hold it down a little, the card players did. Big game going. He was just having a little fun. Nobody got riled up till he shot the good whiskey. Shot it right off the bar."

Noah and the lieutenant traded glances.

"You okay, Private Freeman?"

"Fine, sir. I just thought I knew that man. Guess I was wrong."

"We need to talk, private," the young officer said. "Later."

Noah and the lieutenant turned their attention back to Doodad, whom Noah thought to be an earnest man of sufficient character, but a little strange, as perhaps one who never quite got life's buttons engaged in the right buttonhole. Right away Noah knew Doodad wasn't army material. Like the duty officer said only the day before when Noah signed up: In the army, you live by rules. Ain't always fun, but army rules keep a roof over your head, your belly full, and can get you a pension someday. And rules can keep you alive. "We have rules, we have discipline—you hear me? —discipline," the day officer had said. "We ain't no sloppy-ass civilians playing cowboy and Indians." Clearly the Cactus Saloon and its habitués constituted an establishment in need of discipline.

"Finally," Doodad told the lieutenant, "me and my brother, that's Derwood, had had enough. But they slapped me back and pulled a gun on Derwood, said they was leaving and we all sat back down. That's when the shooter run back in and shot the banjo man. Poor fellow. Right in the middle of a real pretty song, too.

"We all hit the floor and they run off. Rode off east, best I could tell. They better ride fast, too, all I say. Because they made Derwood mad."

Soon things got back to normal in the Cactus Saloon: The girls were teasing, the discount whiskey was flowing, and the card game was shuffling into action, and in the back room of the Cactus Saloon, a father of seven was breathing normally again. Only the music had stopped.

As the lieutenant and Noah left the saloon, Noah said, "Lieutenant, am I right or are my eyes playing tricks—but did that Doodad fellow have his boots on the right feet?"

* * *

The next day Derwood returned to his station at the Cactus Saloon. "Must of chased 'em twenty miles," he told Doodad. "Only got one shot off. And Little Brother, nobody ever slaps you in public like that again, you hear?"

At the fort, Lieutenant Gibson ordered Noah to his quarters. "Private

Freeman, I hardly know you, obviously. But I've seen enough to know you're a cut above most soldiers we get out here." He looked Noah hard in the eye. "The day sergeant says you could read every word on your enlistment form, slight as it is, and you signed your name in script handsome as a schoolmarm's. Mr. Freeman, the army can use a smart man like you. But I've got one question: "What are you running from?"

* * *

In Saint Angela, the street talk could get downright personal and catty, like all good gossip, and the Buck boys, Derwood and Doodad, specialized in playfully wicked rumor. Little in Saint Angela eluded the Bucks, no comings and goings, no shootings or wooings, no nothings or somethings or anythings, for they had presumed squatters' rights to the narrow oak bench outside the Cactus Saloon. It was there, from midmorning to deep into night, that they held forth and traded news and lies with all passersby, town criers without portfolio or guile. They regularly snuck furtive swigs of rotgut, furtive because their poor dead mama always said she'd whup the livin' daylights out of both boys if she ever found them imbibing the Devil's brew in public. Though well into their thirties now, Derwood and Doodad still harbored a saintly respect for Mama's admonitions. But drink they did. Strong drink seemed to chase away the misery of the only work they'd made good at: shoveling dung and hauling stone for Fort Concho and, in the evenings, cleaning spittoons and stopping fights at the Cactus Saloon. It wasn't steady work, except the spittoon-cleaning and fight-stopping, but on a good month the boys could each pull down about $15, a couple of dollars more than an army private made.

It was enough to keep the Bucks in beans and biscuits and an occasional fevered liaison with one of Saint Angela's shanty ladies on Saturday night, Saturday being payday. The brothers made an effective team—like two halves making a whole, many said—with Derwood considered the brains and younger brother Doodad, the sidekick in a pale, soft, even amiable way. In defusing confrontation, Doodad had a natural talent, which he frequently employed in the saloon with a childlike laughter and naiveté that, along with a powerful bear hug, could disarm the most potential combatants. In matters of life, Doodad was known to be generously pliant. Once in San Antonio a dance hall performer of Amazonian proportions separated him from his meager savings and then begged him to marry her. The next morning both his saddle and prospective new wife were gone.

"Guess she couldn't heft your horse," Derwood said.

Derwood—though known as a crack shot who could bring down a scampering deer at 500 yards with his Whitworth rifle—developed a reputation for intellectual prowess: a gift for block-printing his name in perfect ninety-degree angles and poring over an open Bible for hours, never once moving his lips.

"Now that's a sign of real God-given gray matter," proclaimed Pastor James one day while trying to expand his flock at the expense of Cactus Saloon patrons. Of particular note, the traveling preacher and potion hawker said, was Derwood's divine flair for reading the Good Book upside down, a feat the preacher said would probably never be chanced upon more than once. "This man is deep, my brothers, oh so deep. A man of great wisdom. And to bear witness to the Lord there on that bench among so many souls who shall die in hell's eternal flames—it's the mark of a real man. A godly man."

All Derwood knew was that when he left Alabama to fight the Yankees, Mama Buck had given him a leather-bound New Testament and announced that toting Jesus' words in war was the surest way of getting back home alive. Further, she said, a man who stood on good terms with the Scriptures was sure-fire certain to attract a good woman—"one who didn't whore around or take the Lord's name in vain."

At least Derwood got back alive, even if he couldn't read.

* * *

From the day Mary Mills and Duff McNamara rolled into town in their ruby-wheeled wagon, they paid little heed to loose talk or blistering stares. To Mary, the angels had seen fit to bestow upon her a gift of undeniable charm. Eight years earlier Mary lost a baby. Molly Mills, six months old, died of pneumonia, her death coming just a month after the baby's father was killed in the war. Wracked by heartbreak, Mary threw herself into worldly commitment. From her home in Cincinnati she worked tirelessly with the Underground Railroad to free runaway slaves.

Now, surely, here in this wind-lashed and lonely West Texas, as wild and forlorn as any of God's handiwork, she was finally reaping all she'd sown, something now to take away her blues: a baby, a child to hold and dote on and call her own, at least for a little while.

Duff, increasingly smitten by baby gurgles and his own capacity for talking baby talk, was perhaps more intrigued than paternalistic: He'd never seen a colored baby with green eyes, and he'd seen a lot of colored folks in his younger days in St. Louis. After all, his father, an aspiring photographer himself, had often taken Duff to slave auctions on the courthouse steps and down to the landing on the Mississippi to photograph the stevedores and the draymen hauling cargo.

Duff was convinced that Mary was scheming to keep the baby—and for more than just a while. From the moment they found her until they arrived at Fort Concho, Mary held tight to her squirming bundle. At times, Duff noticed, she pulled the baby to her chest and closed her eyes and rocked gently. He wondered what she was thinking, and sensed trouble.

"Mrs. Mills," he said, "it might not be good to get attached to that little girl so."

"Mr. McNamara, I would gladly appreciate it if you'd hush your mouth. We may well be all this baby has."

We? A bracing feeling swept over Duff McNamara, like opening a door on a bitter winter night. He bit even harder on his pipe stem.

"Still and all," he said, "this baby has a mama and daddy somewhere."

"I suppose she might—if they're not dead." Mary remembered all the stories from slaves she helped—of their being caught so close to freedom, then beaten, and sometimes killed on the spot. Slavery was an institution whose reach was as egalitarian as it was virulent; few, whatever their beliefs, escaped its consequences. Her own daddy, whom she idolized, had been a zealous abolitionist in New Orleans before fleeing to more hospitable climes up North. He slipped out of town on the River Queen, a popular steamboat that plied the Mississippi and Ohio rivers.

"The bastards won't get me down," he had assured Mary, the only family member to accompany him on that hastily arranged excursion. "We shall prevail. And one day we'll return home in splendid triumph."

"Father dear," the teenager replied as the paddle-wheeler's gangplank lowered onto the landing at their new home. "You think Cincinnati has any good-looking boys?"

* * *

As the wagon passed through the little outpost of Saint Angela that first afternoon, two men captured Mary Mills' attention: One was lying under a bench in front of the Cactus Saloon, his hat covering his face, a limp hand cupped into the vee of his groin, scratching; the other man sat hunched over a small book, his face hidden by an old slouch hat that only partially obscured a waterfall of blond waves spilling almost onto his chest. The book reader look up, then slapped his companion on the leg. The companion, startled, arose suddenly, whacking his head on the bench's underbelly.

Mary turned her head discreetly so her eyes could follow the two men, in particular the reader. She could not quite hear his words:

"Damnation, Doodad, that bed's bigger than that cow you almost married."

"Maybe better looking, too," Doodad conceded, admiring the intricate carving on the dark-wood headboard.

Neither brother could hear what Mary said to Duff, which was:

"In Texas, the white man is the civilized one, right?"

* * *

He missed Mama Buck, Derwood did.

Nearly a decade earlier, at the dawning of war, Mama Buck had taken to violent coughing fits, clattering spasms that worsened by the week. She saw a specialist in Montgomery—where Derwood was eagerly mustered into the Alabama 59th Infantry as a sharpshooter and Doodad was summarily rejected—but the doctor offered little hope.

"All you can do to treat devil coughs like you got—move to the Southwest," he said. "West Texas. Hot and dry, that's what you need."

Three months later, Mama and Doodad arrived in Saint Angela, a fledgling mecca for consumption victims.

When the war ended, Derwood immediately joined his mother and brother in Texas. Mama Buck became so excited when he walked through the door that early June day that she coughed up bits of bloody tissue and sputum all afternoon. Her hair had turned angel white, and her eyes appeared to Derwood to be holding back tears.

"It's just lung," she said of the red speckling on her linen bedcover. "And Derwood Baby, would you take Mama's cup outside and empty it. She smiled weakly and closed her sad, rheumy eyes. "Thank you, hon."

Derwood could hardly look as he poured the contents of the nearly full sputum cup into a patch of prickly pear.

The next day the boys sat quietly with Mama Buck, whose raspy slumber was but twice abandoned—once when seized by a coughing spell, and once when she summoned Derwood to come near.

He leaned over her bed, his ear practically touching her lips, and hoped that a new salvo of infectious coughs did not explode. In a hoarse half-whisper, she said, "Derwood, hon, promise me you'll always keep a look out for my baby boy. I hold a mighty worry for Doodad. He never was like most boys; he never lost his little boy notions: always saw the good in ever' body, ever' thing. Old hound pee on his leg and he'd call it a spring rain. I know you think I loved him most; maybe I did, but he needed it most, he did. Take care of my baby boy, Derwood. Take care of my baby. I'm awfully tired now."

Derwood pulled away, for all seemed said.

It wasn't. "One more thing." Mama Buck motioned Derwood to listen close. "You don't help him, he won't never amount to a hill of beans."

Doodad all the while had remained at the foot of the bed, head bowed, face in hands, apparently insulated once again from the world about him.

Mama Buck coughed in fits all night. Then she slept peacefully. She was dead by dawn.

* * *

One scorching afternoon three weeks after the arrival of the colored baby, the fetching young white woman, and the odd little photographer who kept telling all within earshot he was destined to capture the ultimate frontier photograph—a real live Indian scalping—Derwood and Doodad's thoughts turned once again to the chatter of Saint Angela.

"A high-dollar whore, I bet—you see that bedstead?" Doodad said.

"All them curlycue carvings?" replied Derwood?

"Regular folk don't have them fancy beds."

"Saw a headboard like that in New Orleans once," said Derwood, a fond smile arching his moustache. "Best buck-fifty I ever spent."

"Kinda made the war worth it, you say?"

"Wouldn't go that far, but sure beat chasing Yankees."

"She gonna have competition here aplenty, Saint Angela, she is,"

"Yeah, she better watch her back, all right," said Derwood. "Them shanty girls can git mean like a nest of scorpions if somebody stealin' their customers."

"I hear she's staying with her sister."

"Maybe they'll open a little business together, Baby Brother—have a two for one on Saturday night."

"Only if no dern cowboys ridin' through," Doodad said.

"Crazy, that sister of hers, I hear. Her soul possessed by the devil himself."

"Flat lost her mind—I hear—over some man never coming back."

"That husband, he was smart, leaving. But taking a herd to California, well, not smart a bit. Lots of wild country between here and California."

"I hear she was a real nag about his drinkin'. Setting fire to his bed that night—and him passed out like a sleeping baby."

"He no more went to California than I can talk French," Derwood said.

"French, why, that's where that fancy bed was made, I bet," Doodad said. "I hear that place's running over with pretty whores."

"France, you ignorant coot."

Derwood, like his Mama had, worried about Baby Brother, about what might happen to Doodad if nobody was around to look after him. What if, Derwood imagined, he himself got struck dead by lightning or thrown from a horse and knocked stupid, or worse? Who would keep Doodad from losing all his money to four-flushing gamblers? Who would tell him he had to clean the dung off his boots? Who would put an arm around his shoulder when the whores laughed at him and took all his money? He couldn't even grow a dashing moustache like Derwood's, the hair on his upper lip too thin and gappy. Doodad had never caught a real break, not from birth: The frail, aging doctor held him overhead—held him by the legs upside down, and as he commenced slapping the tiny buttocks, the old gent's grasp on the placenta-slick, spindly legs failed him. The newborn hit the bed footboard face-first. And then, similarly, the plank floor. It took a good half hour to get the blood scrubbed off everything and baby patched up, just as Mama Buck was asking to see her new child.

When Mama Buck, still drowsy from the pain and medicinal whiskey, took a loving first look at baby, she screamed to high heavens.

"My God, My God, I must be dreaming! What in tarnation has my merciful God wrought?"

"It's your new baby boy, Mrs. Buck," said the doctor. "Fine little specimen, too, ma'am. Fine indeed."

Mama Buck knew better.

"What's that on his head?" she demanded.

"Why, it's his face, Mrs. Buck," the doctor said. .

"But what's that 'doodad! on his face?" She practically spit the offending word.

The baby's face was wrapped in tight strips of bandage, with a large crooked hump where the nose was supposed to be. It appeared as if a mummy-wrap gone bad, his lumpily bandaged head with slits for eyes. "That's where his little nose is, only it not so little right now. Little accident."

"My Lord in Heaven," she said, "his little nose?! I've seen mules with smaller honkers. It's it . . . it's not like a regular nose—it runs east and west! Sea to sea!"

She then collapsed into her pillows in uncontrollable sobs.

"Oh, what will become of him," Mama Buck wailed. "That ugly doodad, oh, that doodad. . . .."

The doctor carried the boogered-up baby into the next room to meet his father, who said, "Mama likes Doodad, Doodad's fine by me."

* * *

"Bear," Quint said, "I know where that nigger Noah is."

Bear Coltrain wasn't surprised, knowing how determined Quint was to get even with those whose will he couldn't break.

"He joined the army."

Bear had heard talk since the killing of Jake Pratt—that old man Pratt had a hand in nigger Noah's disappearance. "I hear Pratt's friends took up a collection to help. Word gets around in this town."

"Yeah, and one of the fellas he hit up for money squealed—said that old Jake wanted to help his friend Noah start a new life, mos' likely the army."

"About the only place around here a colored can find a new life."

"The sheriff and I go way back—our Mississippi days. He was as good a slave tracker as I ever saw. Good as me, almost. And, boy, could he give them a beatin'.

"Anyways, I had my boys split up, scout out all the line forts west—looking for a new Fort Worth nigger."

"Green-eyed boy."

"Kinda hated to do up old Jake, but he had it coming," said Quint Carpenter as he and Bear relaxed in a saloon behind the Fort Worth courthouse. "How he could take that beating—why hell fire, I coulda been picking off his kids one by one right in front of him and I don't think he'd never told me a thing."

"Never even yelped when you busted his legs, I hear."

"You hear right. So hard-headed we finally put a couple of bullets in him to make sure he knew we was serious."

"Well, what do we do now?"

"We're gonna lay low a couple a days," Quint said, a menacing smile contorting his face. "My boys found that green-eye at Concho. We'll be paying a visit out there real soon. Care to join us?"

"I'd be mighty pleased to join you," Bear said.

"Another whiskey, barkeep."

"Hardest nigger to kill dead I ever saw," said Bear. "How does it feel to get outsmarted by a slave nigger so long, Mr. Sheriff?"

"Them days over."

They ordered still more whiskey and began making plans.

"Never yelped once," Quint muttered, sounding almost, but not quite, impressed.

* * *

Duff McNamara loved the flat, treeless prairie around Saint Angela. Should any Indians decide to attack, he thought, you could see them coming for miles and prepare. Duff had decided to remain in Saint Angela for a while so he could photograph what he had not found in Fort Worth—the most historic shots possible in the American frontier. In Duff's mind, that meant he wanted to take pictures of real Indians doing real Indian things, like warriors bringing down buffalo with arrows and squaws hauling papooses on their backs and smoke curling from teepees and old men sitting around the campfire smoking communal pipes. But should the Indians not be inclined to pose peacefully, he'd settle for the images of a good marauding party in which somebody gets a head-skinning. A scalping—the ultimate great photograph of the frontier, which he knew he could only obtain two ways: make friends with the Indians who practiced the art of scalping or go out on his own and hope for the best.

He could sell it to newspapers and magazines back East—maybe *Harper's!*—and find the fame and fortune that eluded him in St. Louis.

As a youth still learning his craft, he had a chance to capture a truly historic moment in 1861: a slave auction in his hometown of St. Louis.

Duff had long been familiar with the courthouse, having as a five-year-old accompanied his father to that very building for the first of the Dred Scott trials in 1847. A decade later the Supreme Court decision ruling against Scott, denying his freedom and voiding the Missouri Compromise, became one of the events that led to the Civil War.

Duff had prepared well for that 1861 auction. All his equipment was in place and checked. He had attended auctions with his father, whose photography equipment he inherited. He knew the routine—the slaves brought shackled to the top of the steps on the courthouse's Fourth Street side; they were then presented for inspection to bidders as family members begged to be sold together; and finally came the tears and cries of separation of husbands and wives and children, and all the while, on the side, old men prayed earnest prayers beseeching mercy on their souls. Great drama, Duff knew. Great history. Great photograph.

As usual, the crowd gathered early for the trafficking in human commerce. But this time was different: The crowd was far larger as it pressed ever closer to the courthouse steps. Spectators jostled Duff and knocked his camera and tripod from its scaffolding. The yelling and catcalls grew louder, drowning out the auctioneers. Some two thousand demonstrators shouted for the auction to stop, which it did, finally. It would be the last slave auction held in St. Louis and, Duff believed, his last chance to get the great American photograph.

That's when Duff McNamara decided to head west, to Fort Worth and the real frontier. No more chronicling the countenances of wealthy German immigrants. Ever.

Yet, now, in Saint Angela, Duff had yet to fulfill his dream, or even to begin chasing it: He was staying with Mrs. Mills and her sister, Constance, in the sister's two-room adobe home that sat a scant quarter-mile upriver from the Fort Concho. If West Texas were to give up its promise of fame and fortune, it sure seemed far away. His environment was hardly inspiring. (What the hell, Duff concluded, maybe I should lower my sights; maybe I'll just try to get a photograph of the most authentic saloon shootout I can find.) The baby consumed Mrs. Mills' attention all day and her sister, well, Mrs. Mills was right about her sister, he thought: Her faculties never did gallop at top speed. For most of the day all she did was fret about how dusty her dirt floor was, and come mid-afternoon she moved an old rocking chair with a rope-broke seat to the west side of her house, facing the sun, staring over a horizon she found as barren as her heart. Whenever Duff approached her, which was often, she said, "He should be getting back any time now." She would be rocking, very slowly. Sometimes she rocked all night, silhouetted in the cold moon glow.

Chapter Eight

by Mary Dittoe Kelly

The saloon in Fort Worth where Quint and Bear Coltrain were discussing their plans to kill Noah was fairly quiet. It was a bit too early in the day to attract anyone but the serious drinkers or those wanting to talk the kind of business that didn't belong in an office or eating establishment. The exception, of course, was when a trail drive arrived. Then the cowhands would burst into the saloon like the crazy herd they'd just corralled. Some would be fractious, some horny as a teaser stud in a pen full of mares. Trail dust would fill the air, slapped off their clothes as they headed for the bar. When the cowhands arrived, prudent men often decided they could skip that day's libations.

But this was not one of those days. Bear and Quint took up one table. Across the saloon, three well-dressed men were having a quiet discussion, and the long bar had a few solitary drinkers. One of them was seated close enough to Bear and Quint to be distracted by their coarse, self-satisfied conversation. At first he tried to ignore them, then thought of moving farther down the bar. Until he heard something that changed his mind and focused his attention on their every word.

The declaration that caught the lone man's ear was, "Bear, I know where that nigger Noah is." The two men continued with their boastful conversation. The one named Quint was bragging about having some sheriff in his pocket, saying they went back a ways to their slave tracking days in Mississippi. Quint allowed that the sheriff was almost as good a slave catcher as he was, and sure knew how to beat a nigger almost to death.

* * *

The man at the bar involuntarily clenched his fists when Quint told his friend Bear that the "green-eyed nigger" had been found by his boys, that he was stationed at Fort Concho, and they'd be riding out in a few days to kill him.

The listener noticed that the remarks of the man named Bear were calculated. He seemed to enjoy riling up Quint's hatred of this man, Noah. At one point he asked, "How does it feel to get outsmarted by a slave nigger for so long?" Bear either hated all coloreds or he had some particular reason of his own for wanting this one colored man dead.

Surreptitiously, the man at the bar took the whiskey he'd been nursing and poured it down his shirt front. He then called out loudly to the bartender, intentionally slurring his words, "Hey, what's it take for a man to get him another drink in here? My money not good enough for you?" When the bartender brought the bottle, the man said, loud enough for the benefit of those around him, "Hit me twice, so I don't have to wait for your sorry ass when I'm ready for the next one."

Again, he poured most of the drink down his shirt front. Then he said, to no one in particular, "There's gotta be a better place to get a drink than this shit hole." With that, he downed his whiskey in one swallow and pushed away from the bar. As he turned to leave, he stumbled, bumping into the table with the two men hard enough to spill their drinks. Before they had time to get mad, the man shouted for the bartender again. "Hey Molasses," he slurred, "get your sorry ass over here so's I can buy my friends here a bottle." He began to pull bills out of his pocket, weaving slightly on his feet. "Gennlemen, I humbly beg your pardon." His blurry gaze passed over each of the men as he doled out his money on their table; it gave him just enough time to memorize their faces. "It's my leg, ya know, gives out on me once inna while, got shot a while back, ain't never been quite right since then." With a drunk's exaggerated flourish, he tipped his hat, bowed from the waist, and left the bar, bumping a few more tables on his way.

Once outside the saloon, John Howard Malone quickly made his way to the livery stable. He instructed the man there to get his horse ready and to pack enough feed to last the animal during a journey of several days. His next stop was the general store, where he did the same for himself, purchasing jerky, hardtack, and coffee. Then he went to the boardinghouse where he'd been staying and quickly packed his few belongings. Within the hour, Malone was on his way to Fort Concho.

A green-eyed black man named Noah—there was just too much coincidence not to check it out. Noah was the name of the green-eyed escaped slave who had risked his own life on the battlefield to save Malone's. But Malone liked Noah for more reasons than that. Sure, he owed him, and in Malone's code of honor, that in itself was enough. But beyond that, he had developed a real affection for Noah over the months they spent together in the field. Malone and Preacher John had taught him to read when there was enough of a lull in the fighting. They had talked into the night around the campfire. Malone liked Noah, and respected him. If Noah's life needed saving, Malone would save it or die trying.

* * *

Lieutenant Thomas Blaine Gibson was an educated man from Pennsylvania and given to the pursuit of history and philosophy. He had been stationed at Fort Concho for almost six months now, and he knew the buffalo soldiers were despised by many of the locals who still resented the outcome of the Civil War. There were white men under his command who didn't feel much different. But Gibson had been raised by parents who were staunch abolitionists, and he had been taught from a young age to despise the atrocities of slavery.

This Noah Freeman, facing him now, was no ordinary soldier. He had come in to Saint Angela riding a buckskin gelding that any man would covet, a big horse with the girth and legs to carry a man as tall and strong as Noah. And Noah carried the bill of sale for the horse, which he rode with a gentle hand. In fact, for a man of Noah's stature and obvious strength, Gibson had quickly sensed that he was not prone to violence.

And Noah Freeman could read and write. Lieutenant Gibson was intrigued by this. Noah's soft drawl pegged him as a southerner, so surely he had been a slave. Where did he learn to read and write so well?

Gibson and Noah were in the lieutenant's quarters, having returned from the altercation at the Cactus Saloon, an event that somehow involved the new private. Gibson directed Noah to a chair, and the big man settled his bulk without comment. His face was hard to read—not sullen at all, but neither was there any show of eagerness to please. Gibson knew that Noah had secrets, and it was Gibson's job to extract those secrets, to satisfy himself that Noah was not involved in something that could bring danger to the other troops. On some level, Gibson already knew that would not be the case. He sensed an integrity in Noah that would not be compromised. But, whatever the situation was, he needed to know. Once again, he asked Noah, "Private, what are you running from?"

Noah had heard his lieutenant's question the first time. He wasn't being disrespectful. More than anything, he felt himself to be frozen up, like a water trough after a West Texas blizzard. He just couldn't seem to come up with any words that would cause his mouth to open. On the ride back to the fort, his intuition about the man he'd run after outside the saloon had finally kicked in. He was one of the posse that rode with Quint and his boys, possessed of the same meanness they displayed, meanness that existed just for its own sake.

The knowledge of this was what had him feeling like he was inside a big block of ice. He didn't feel angry, nor afraid, nor in a rush to move on again, to find a safe place. Because now he understood there was no safe place. Until the day they killed him, he would be pursued by Quint or Bear Coltrain, or both. The truth was obvious: Taking everything from Noah—his wife, his family, his homestead—none of this was enough to satisfy them. Here he was out in the middle of nowhere, no harm to Quint or Coltrain, yet still they pursued him like the hounds of hell.

Noah was tired of running. Standing up for himself had only brought him suffering, yet now it was certain that running would only bring more of the same. No more running, ever. He was prepared to stay right where he was until Quint or Coltrain and their vicious sidekicks came riding in, or even return to Fort Worth to confront them. Noah just didn't care. He had lost everything dear to him, and now it seemed he had finally lost his very own self. It would be so much better to finally get things over with, even if his own death was the result.

Freedom. He had fought so hard to get it. The government told him he had it. But hadn't he lost everything dear to him by living "free" among the Quints and Coltrains of the world? If freedom was a double-edged sword, he had fallen on its wrong side too many times.

The lieutenant poured two short glasses of brandy and pulled a chair up close to Noah's. He'd seen this look of resignation on the battlefield, the look that said "Death holds no fear for me. I stand to welcome it." Gibson held the glass of brandy to Noah's lips. "Drink this," he commanded gently.

The brandy burned down Noah's throat. His story was so tragic, and would take so long to tell. But his commanding officer had commanded him to respond, and he had to obey.

"Sir, seems like I've been runnin' all my life, from one thing or t'other. So I don't exactly know how to answer your question if you want to know the truth." He looked into his lieutenant's eyes and saw only kindness, the like of which he'd not seen in a white man since the time he'd spent under Captain Malone's command. Gibson, Noah sensed, was cut from the same cloth as the other officer. "Lieutenant, sir, where would you like me to start?"

The lieutenant sat back down and poured Noah another brandy. "Well, why don't you just start at the beginning and we'll see where that takes us."

* * *

Mary Mills wasn't sure just which of several possibilities the town gossips were chewing on the most, savoring every last morsel, she was sure. And she was just as sure that the juiciest gossip revolved around her!

Why, just look at the possibilities. First, there was Constance, rocking on that porch all the day long, talking to her husband like he was standing right in front of her. Only coming to live in town because the army forced her to. "Truthfully," Mary had muttered to Duff McNamara just that morning, "I will be as surprised as the next person if that man ever comes back!"

Duff had shaken his head in agreement. "Your sister needs a large dose of medicine—in her case, the truth. You need to get her skinny behind up outta that rocker so you can look her in the eye and state the facts. That husband is not coming back; I guarantee it. Put a shovel in the woman's hand and get her to planting some beans and taters, so she doesn't starve to death come winter."

Mary Mills knew Duff was right, but so far, she couldn't bring herself to address the matter with Constance. "Best to just leave her to enjoy that fog she's in for a while longer."

The truth of the matter (and Mary Mills felt shame to know this about herself) was that she was glad that Constance took no notice of things around her. Why, if Constance were to sit up and take it all in, she'd raise the roof just to get a strange man and a colored baby out from under it! Mary would just let the gossips go on about her addled sister for a while yet.

And yes, if she had any interest in propriety herself, what woman would allow a man not her kin to eat and sleep inside her house without a husband to oversee the matter? Goodness, Mary herself had spilled the beans about Duff McNamara just last week, when she was in Urban's General Store contemplating some purchases. The storekeep's wife had sashayed right up, bold as brass, to ask her, did she want to take home some tobacco for her husband?

Caught off guard, Mary had responded forcefully, "Mr. Duff McNamara is not my husband, Mrs. Urban!" Immediately, she saw that she had fallen right into the woman's trap. All innocent looking, Mrs. Urban had asked, "Oh, then, how is it that you are related?" Mary Mills knew the sudden flush she felt rise to her cheeks was the reward the nosy woman had been hoping for.

"He is not my husband, and no, he is not kin to my sister and me. We have offered him temporary lodging because he is helping us with some business matters that are of the utmost personal concern." Stressing the word "personal" she had fixed her blue eyes on Mrs. Urban's pinched face, as much as daring her to ask what that business might be.

Before the town magpie could open her mouth, Mary continued, "You must pardon me. I have tarried and will be late for an appointment." And she had turned on her heel and walked out, head held high and not one single thing on her list purchased! She intended to rectify that situation today.

Really, why should she care what they were saying about her and Duff

McNamara? Mary had no intention of staying in this godforsaken settlement forever. A month or so, to build up Constance's strength for the journey, and Mary would be taking her back to Cincinnati where there were good doctors and other marks of true civilization. If she and Duff were wrong and her sister's husband did in fact return, he knew Constance had a sister in Cincinnati. He could just come and get his wife in Ohio, or maybe even decide to settle there with her.

So, as far as Mary was concerned, the town gossips could have her and Duff McNamara carrying on like those fancy girls and dirty cowboys she'd seen entering and leaving the Right Hotel at all hours. She'd be gone before she knew anyone well enough to care what they thought. It was just that nosy Mrs. Urban caught Mary off guard; that was the only reason Mary had felt herself blushing so. People without the social graces, that's all these Saint Angela residents were.

But of all the gossip fodder she provided, Mary Mills suspected there was one piece chewed on far longer than the others, and that piece was ... Baby. The very same baby that she carried in her arms this moment, on her way back to the store to buy the dry goods not purchased last week.

Let them all stare! Let them all imagine her burning in the hellfire of God's damnation. Mary knew the truth: Baby would have died within hours had Mary not heard her cries. She had saved a life, just as sure as she had saved lives working the Underground Railroad in Ohio. And if she cared to, she just might tell someone the God's truth about how she rescued Baby. She might even tell that nosy Mrs. Urban, right now today, if she asked another impertinent question.

Baby...that's what she had taken to calling the little angel, and Duff had followed suit. Colored or not, this was one of the most beautiful babies Mary had ever seen. A smile hardly ever left her face, not even in sleep, and when she looked at you with those big green eyes the color of springtime...why, anyone's heart would melt!

Caring for Baby had lit a fire inside Mary Mills she thought had been extinguished for good when she lost her husband and child just weeks apart. Those losses dried her up inside. And then God arranged for her to find Baby by the river, just like Moses in the bulrushes, she was sure of it. The knowledge that the Good Lord Himself had wanted Mary to find

Baby, that was what caused her to feel so protective, knowing she was acting according to God's will.

Baby…that was her name for now. But Mary was already thinking of other names for her beautiful child, once they were back in Ohio. The two names she'd been pondering the last few days were Avril and Hope. Avril was the French word for the month of April, the full-blooming time of spring, which is when she'd found Baby. It seemed to be a name that held a lot of promise of good things to come. And the other name she liked was Hope, for obvious reasons.

She would raise Baby up with all the love she'd had for her own child. She would teach her everything she knew—not just reading and writing, but piano, and poetry, and philosophy, and how to be a gracious hostess. She would raise Baby up to be a leader for her own people to admire and emulate. She would raise Baby up to show that there was hope for everybody in this world.

Avril Hope Mills…yes, it had the right ring to it. Mary thought she may have found the perfect name. So wrapped up was she in her thoughts of the future that she had forgotten to take heed of the slippery spots that last night's much needed rain had brought to the dirt street and boardwalk of Saint Angela. Placing her foot on a slick spot, Mary went down hard, and Baby flew out of her arms.

Derwood and Doodad were the first to see the spill from their post outside the Cactus Saloon. They hastened to give aid to the woman and child. It just seemed natural that Derwood would go to the woman's side while Doodad went straight to the child. Doodad was happy to see that the little colored baby had landed face up in a fragrant mix of mud and recently dropped horse manure. What luck to end up on such a soft cushion!

Doodad looked down on Baby, who apparently thought being tossed through the air was a wonderful new game. She was laughing and reaching out to Doodad as if to say, "Do that again!" Doodad picked the baby up, and she smiled at him with all the trust in the world. Doodad smiled back, oblivious to the mud and manure blending in with his already fragrant clothing, and the baby rewarded him with a happy gurgle, her big green eyes sparkling with delight. Doodad felt his heart begin to melt.

Mary Mills regained consciousness to the smells of tobacco, manure, and perfumed body water. She instantly screamed, "Baby, Baby!" and tried to rise, but was pushed back down by a piercing pain in her skull and the gentle hands of Doc Tibbs. "The child is fine," he said reassuringly, "You just need to lie back down." Mary drifted back into unconsciousness, and Doc Tibbs looked with satisfaction at the best nursemaid he could imagine for the child, a hopelessly smitten Doodad Buck.

* * *

Noah had been riding south and west for two days now. The map Lieutenant Gibson had given him was very accurate. He was constantly watching out for Indians, Mexican bandits, and American outlaws, but so far his only enemies had been of a different species. He had given a wide detour to an eight foot rattler that had been sunning itself on a rock until the sound of his horse's hooves had caused it to give a warning rattle. And he had shaken an angry scorpion out of his boot this morning, but these were just normal encounters in West Texas.

After they had spent most of the night talking, Lieutenant Gibson had called for the stable boy to rig a mule with provisions to last for several weeks. He had sent Noah off riding north from Fort Concho, with instructions to turn in a southwesterly direction come daybreak.

After hearing Noah's story, the lieutenant's primary objective was to keep Noah out of harm's way until he figured out his next move, or as circumstances dictated. He wouldn't take the chance that one of his own men might rat out a comrade if there was money involved. The spread he put out was that Noah was headed northwest on a scouting expedition. In fact, Noah was heading for Fort Stockton, where the Ninth Cavalry was currently stationed. He carried a letter from Lieutenant Gibson to the Fort Stockton commander. The letter stated that Noah was an admirable recruit and that he needed to be out of Saint Angela for a while. The letter recommended that Noah be put to work busting horses.

By his calculations, Noah would reach Fort Stockton in another three or four days. He wasn't anxious to get there. Why was it, he wondered, that he had agreed to the lieutenant's plan rather than follow his initial impulse to return to Fort Worth for a final showdown with his longtime enemies? He was also surprised to find an unusual solace on this long ride. Unusual, because being alone these days just made it harder to not think about Nelly, his sons, and his lost baby girl who was dead or alive, he didn't know.

Noah had a lot to think about other than just making it alive to Fort Stockton. Talking all night to Lieutenant Gibson was an experience Noah couldn't quite figure out. Somehow, every time Noah had tried to end his story, the lieutenant had asked him another question that carried Noah back to another time of his life, another episode when he had just been looking for freedom. The questions ended when Noah told of Lovie's kidnapping, the deaths of Nelly and his two boys, and his own near death, and how he'd gotten to Saint Angela because of Jake Pratt's kindness. When he got to that part, his voice had faltered, and he had succumbed again to the fatigue of his despair.

Now, as he rode on under the blistering Texas sun, Noah suddenly realized something. Never before had he told one person about his whole life, as far back as he could remember. He'd been embarrassed talking so much, but each time he tried to defer, the lieutenant had bored down on him like a branding iron on a heifer. Now, in the vast stillness of the plains, Noah was revisiting his past and realizing, in spite of his grievous losses, that he had also told the lieutenant about some good things in his life. He had ridden a very long way to get from Mississippi to Texas, and he had encountered good worth remembering, as well as the bad, along the way.

Good and generous people, people deserving to have their stories told, had helped him accomplish his dream, nightmare that it now was. Lieutenant Gibson had forced him to remember every single one of them. Though Noah had never known his father and had lost his mother when he was sold at age eleven, he now was able to see how many others had cared for him in a fashion that was every bit as loving as the way he had cared for his own boys and his lost baby Lovie, and his sister Lovie too, for the short time he had her back in his life.

This long ride he was on seemed to invite further reflection on all those who had helped him get this far. As he recalled them, he felt inclined to say a prayer for each, asking God to bless them for their generous hearts and to protect them from harm, if they were still alive. He hoped their stories had turned out better than his.

The first help he'd gotten on his search for freedom was from Uncle Jonah, after Noah had killed Goliath. He and Aunt Suse had sent Noah into the night with a mule and provisions, a sure death sentence from Massa Ellerbee if he found them out. Next was George and his wife, who had risked their lives to find him safe passage on a boat that could get him to the Union side of Vicksburg.

Some of Noah's most fervent prayers centered on Preacher John, who'd been the closest thing to a father Noah had ever known. Preacher John tutored him in the history of the country at war, taught him that coloreds would eventually fight alongside the white Union soldiers. And wasn't Noah doing that, enlisted in an army that now accepted black men?

Preacher John had also saved Noah from the clutches of Bear Coltrain, when that man was conniving to desert the army and take Noah too, to get hard cash for him on Coltrain's way back home. Preacher John and Noah had proved themselves adept at supporting the Union troops, cooking, busting horses, scouting, tracking, and even some doctoring, using the healing herbs they had been taught to recognize as children. And it was Preacher John, along with the white officer, John Howard Malone, who had taught Noah to read and write. Noah felt a wave of affection wash over him at the thought of these two men, and it was followed by a wave of guilt that he hadn't kept them in his thoughts and prayers the way they deserved. Yes, he had saved Malone's life, but that had not been the reason Malone concerned himself with educating Noah. He had done that out of pure goodness, knowing how hard it would be for Noah to actually be free if he couldn't read nor write.

When Quint and Coltrain burned out his family and left Noah for dead, Mama Lou and Uncle Daniel had nursed him back to life. Not really life, for the spirit had been drained clear out of him, and he felt unable to bear his losses. But Mama Lou would not let him give up. Her fierce will proved stronger than his, and he remembered the words she had spoken to him, telling him how wrong he was to think his life was over. "You just started your ride," she'd told him. And she and Uncle Daniel had pushed him to ask his good friend Jake Pratt for help.

After Lieutenant Gibson had run out of questions and Noah had run out of story, the lieutenant got up and paced back and forth for a while before sitting back down. He refreshed their brandies and studied Noah before he spoke.

"Noah, good and evil don't have a color, not black, not brown, not red nor white. But all colors have good and evil; it's the way of the world and not much you nor I can do to change that. Why, just think about Goliath, as cruel as any slave catcher and maybe worse, because he chose to be mean to his own kind, just to benefit himself. Not caring about anyone other than himself, that was Goliath's sin, and he certainly won't be the last like that."

The lieutenant paused, as if measuring his words. "Bear Coltrain, his evil comes from greed, pure and simple. He wants you dead because you've got a piece of good pasture land by the river that he wants for himself."

And as for Quint, well, Lieutenant Gibson thought on Quint for his longest measure before describing Quint in a way Noah had never considered, "Quint is pure evil, there is no denying it. And he will probably stay that way right through his last breath on this earth. No one should make excuses for an evil man like that, but I can't help but wonder how exactly did he get that way? Was he born evil, the fruit of evil parents? Or did he become evil over time, because evil somehow got into him like the worms get into a barrel of apples and turn them all putrid and rotten?" He went on to say that he was making no excuses for Quint; the man had lived long enough to know he had choices.

Gibson added, "Your description of Quint reminds me of a powerful story my father once told me. He had met a man who had been raised by the Indians for half his life, and just like we are doing now, they were having a discussion regarding the good and evil in this world. This man told my father a story about how one of the elders of his tribe had explained good and evil to him when he was a young boy.

"The wise man had told the boy, 'My son, in the heart of every man there live two wolves. One wolf represents goodness and all we know to be true of Mother Earth. The other wolf lives in darkness and represents the evil in the world of men, with all its trappings of pride, greed, and lust. These two wolves inside each of us battle for our spirits, until one is dead and the other the winner.'

"The boy had asked his elder, 'Grandfather, which wolf is going to win my spirit?' and the elder had replied, 'The one you feed, my son.'"

Gibson and Noah sat in silence until the lieutenant continued. "Noah, the evil wolf has gotten a hold on Quint's very soul, because that's the one he's been feeding all his life. He's a man driven by his anger and self-loathing. You can't see it, but he's in a prison of his own making, and he'll never be free."

As Noah rode on, dusk began to settle in, and he knew he'd best be searching for a place to bed down for the night. He thought about the lieutenant's words once again. Quint was in prison and would never be free? The words rang true: Why else would Quint make killing Noah his life's mission? He couldn't tolerate the thought that Noah had eluded him in Mississippi, and even worse, the idea that Noah could settle in Texas and be free.

Something in that thought caused Noah to allow the lieutenant to send him to Fort Stockton, and his long ride had served up the solitude for him to remember his own wise elders. Noah wondered—could it be that God's plan for him was to live with his pain, so that he could someday be a wise elder for the generations to follow? Was it their freedom, not his, that should matter most to him? Suddenly, he remembered the words of the fortune teller: "Don't trade redemption for revenge." Was this thinking leading him on the path to redemption?

* * *

The day after Noah rode out from Fort Concho, Lieutenant. Gibson made it his business to find Derwood and Doodad, who was looking even happier than usual in his light-headed way. He wanted to hear every last detail about the group who had shot up the Cactus Saloon looking for "a green-eyed nigger." Derwood was the one with the eye for detail, and he went back over the events of the night to the lieutenant's satisfaction. Gibson was now convinced that these men had ridden in from Fort Worth looking for Noah Freeman. Now that he was sure, he knew sending Noah to Fort Stockton was not a permanent fix. Figuring out what to do with this knowledge was going to be his next challenge. Thanking the boys, he mounted and turned his horse back toward the fort.

"Wait, lieutenant!" shouted Doodad with a grin from ear to ear, "Don't you want to meet our little green-eyed colored baby?"

Chapter Nine

by Jane Roberts Wood

Lieutenant Gibson had taken four steps before the gist of what Doodad said registered. He wheeled around. "Doodad, what did you just say to me?"

Doodad was hovering over a baby who was sitting in the middle of the dusty road. Taking one of the baby's hands in each of his own, "C'mon now. Show the lieutenant you can walk. Take a step now," he coaxed. Gently, he pulled the baby to her feet. "Take a step and you can have a sugar tit." Then to no one in particular, "Needs a cheer," he mumbled.

"Doodad, what did you say?"

"Always sitting in the dirt, baby needs a cheer."

Lieutenant Gibson leaned over and picked up the baby. Holding her at arm's length, he looked into her round green eyes. Unblinkingly, she stared back at him. Solemnly, she studied his face, tracing his features with her hands. Suddenly, she lurched backward, sending the lieutenant into a scramble of flailing hands and raised knees to keep from dropping her. "Whoa! Whoa now, little baby," he said, taking a firm hold so that she was stretched out on her stomach, lying between two big hands. Unfazed, the baby stared at the ground.

Doodad put a hand over his mouth and giggled. "She ain't never been that far off the ground before," he said. "How tall are you, Lieutenant?"

"Six feet, three inches. Well, now wait a minute here. I've some questions. What's her name?"

"Baby. We just call her Baby."

"Another green-eyed baby girl? I don't believe it. Whose child is she?"

"I reckon she's Miz Mary Mills baby. Miz Mary fell, and I caught the baby."

"Where is Mrs. Mills now?"

"She's laid up, and I'm taking care of Baby. Derwood's helping," and after a pause, "helping some," he added, his brow deeply furrowed.

"So this is Mrs. Mills' little colored baby. I've heard about this child."

"Miz Mary, she's a right fanatic about her little colored baby."

"I know this baby's daddy," Lieutenant Gibson said. "Her true name is Lovie, and this baby means the world and all that's in it to that man. Where can I find Mrs. Mills?"

* * *

A half an hour later, here they were on Doc Tibbs front porch, the three of them, Lieutenant Gibson in a rocking chair, with Lovie sound asleep on his shoulder, and Doodad sitting on the steps just below. Doc Tibbs was nowhere in sight. But enough time had passed so that the order of relationships between the three had been rearranged. Lieutenant Gibson had promoted himself to chief nursemaid, and Doodad, Lovie's willing slave, had proudly become the lieutenant's errand boy. The first errand Doodad had been sent on was to fetch a dozen soft, old flour sacks from the company's storeroom. Lovie's bottom was now as "pure as the driven snow," said Doodad.

"Driven flour," said Gibson.

When all the errands were done—a bottle, warm milk from a cow or goat, "Whatever's easiest," Gibson ordered, and bacon grease for Lovie's chapped lips—the lieutenant began to relax. As the youngest of four back home in Pennsylvania, he had never paid much attention to babies. But with Lovie on his shoulder, soft and feeling like she had not one bone in her body and sweating so that tiny beads of perspiration curved across her forehead, he took note of how warm and oatsy she smelled. Why, she smelled pleasant, like corn in silk and tassel in the fields back home or the flank of a new born calf or a lamb's soft coat. In spite of the fact that she really wasn't all that clean, not all over clean, she smelled nice. The hem of her yellow dress was muddy red, and her face was smudged with dirt, but when Doc Tibbs came they would remedy that. They would fix her up as nice as any white child before her daddy saw her.

At this thought, his heart took a plunge so sudden that he put his hand protectively over it. God almighty! He had sent a man off across the plains, a man who believed he had nothing left to live for. Gibson had no idea where Noah might be at this moment. He hoped he was well on his way to Fort Stockton, but with nothing but an old map drawnby an army lieutenant in 1847, Noah could become confused. But since the route from Concho to Fort Stockton was on the Butterfield Stage line and the Emigrants' Trail, he should make it to Fort Stockton if he didn't die of thirst or run into hostile Indians. A scout had come in yesterday to say the Kiowa were riding, although the scout, Little Six Stars, said it was a peaceful ride, not a war party. However, a lone man with a good horse and a provisioned mule would be easy prey for hungry Indians or Mexican revolutionaries or outlaws. Anybody. After all, the Pecos area between Castle Gap and Fort Stockton lay along what somebody had called "the Comanche War Trail" that led them to raids into Mexico. If he ran into Indians, what chance would Noah have? It would be a damn shame if Noah were to die not knowing he still had part of his family.

Doodad, sitting on the steps at their feet, was feeling squirmy. The straps of his gray overalls had slipped from his bare shoulders that were turning a watermelon pink. And he felt right hungry and thirsty, too. Hooking his thumbs under the straps of his overalls, Doodad repositioned them, stood and tiptoed toward the two in the rocking chair.

"Watch out for that hole," Gibson whispered, nodding toward a varmint hole in Doc Tibbs' porch.

Nodding, Doodad tiptoed around it and put his mouth close to the lieutenant's ear. "Lieutenant, I'm gonna eat a bite and make Baby that cheer," he said in a fast whisper.

Gibson looked at him through slanted eyelids. "What?"

"Me and Derwood. We're gonna make Baby a cheer."

"Good work, Doodad. Good work," Gibson mumbled and, with a wave of his hand, shooed Doodad off.

He watched as the man, his shoulders hunched up around his neck, jumped off the porch and trotted across the rust-colored, dusty road in such a hurry that he broke into a skip now and then. "Like a girl," Gibson told himself, smiling, when Doodad had disappeared into the dark shadows of the livery stable, cattycorner across the street, Gibson closed his eyes and sighed, a long, deeply satisfying, sigh.

"No point in fretting about Noah now," he told himself and put his head back in order to more fully enjoy the enforced rocking-chair rest. Holding the sleeping baby and enjoying the sun that was now a red ball fixed in the western sky, he felt as contented as he'd been lately, so contented that he found himself lazily ignoring the comments made by the soldiers passing along the road.

In a kind of happy, derisive little singsong, the comments went like this: "Hey Lieutenant, where'd you get that little pickaninny?" And, "You been promoted, Lieutenant? You a nursemaid now?" And "The baby sure looks like you!" And the most insulting, and this from the only other lieutenant stationed at Concho, "Well, now, Lieutenant Gibson," Lieutenant Baker drawled, "I do believe you're turning soft." Fighting words any other time, but now Gibson's only acknowledgement of the hazing was to raise the index finger of the hand that held Lovie's head close against his neck and grin.

He closed his eyes. He swatted away a fly buzzing around his head. He was vaguely aware of muffled footsteps crisscrossing the road, sounding sharper on the steps and melding into a hollow sound on the wooden walkway in front of Doc's home office. As a precaution, Gibson inched his chair farther away from the small varmint hole, folded himself comfortably in the chair, stretched his legs out in front of him, crossed his feet at the ankles, and allowed his head to rest partly on Lovie's soft curls. The far off neighing of a horse and the call of a roadrunner were the last sounds he heard before he slept.

Sleeping, he dreamed. In the dream he saw Noah searching, searching, all the while roaming the south plains of Texas. A sandstorm blew in, and now he was riding double with Noah, and then he and Noah were blinded by sand, blowing so thick it turned night into day. And even as he dreamed he somehow knew it was a dream. He woke from the dream, rubbing his eyes. Dazed and only half awake, he rose to his feet, thus setting off a catastrophic response as Lovie rolled out of his lap, down his long legs and dropped soundlessly into the hole.

"Good God, Lovie," he shouted, falling to his knees, "Lovie!" he shouted again, peering into the darkness of the hole.

The clink of spurs and boots on the walkway signaled a passing soldier.

Without taking his eyes off the hole, he hollered, "Soldier, we need help here. Get some men. Sound the alarm!"

Immediately, the call to arms was bugled. Gibson jumped to his feet. "Put down that bugle! I'm countermanding that order. I didn't know it was you, Corporal. The fort is not under attack. We need some help here. Get more men. Sound the alarm. No, not that alarm," he said, as the bugle was raised again. "We've got to find this baby."

Lieutenant Gibson's face was red. He ran down the steps and up them again. He fell to his knees, calling "Lovie! Lovie!" and then it was down the steps and up them again.

Watching the lieutenant's frantic behavior and hearing him calling out what sounded to his ears like the word love repeatedly, the corporal slowly came to the realization that he had stumbled upon a lieutenant gone mad. Clearly, Lieutenant Gibson had lost his senses, and it was commonly known that lieutenants didn't have much sense to begin with. He decided the order of the day was to take charge of this crazy lieutenant.

He crossed his arms. "Lieutenant Gibson, sir! I don't see a baby."

"Of course, you don't see a baby. The baby is in this hole."

"Now, Lieutenant. Sir! Why do you think a baby is in this hole? I do see the hole, sir! Is the baby that you say is in the hole, your baby?"

"You idiot! Get some men in here. That's an order!"

The lieutenant fell to his knees again. Cupping his hands around his eyes, he peered into the hole. His "Lovie! Lovie, you all right?" was met by a silence deeper than that in Lincoln's tomb. The lieutenant jumped to his feet again, ran up and down the steps and, again, fell to his knees calling "Lovie! Lovie!"

A man looking for love in a varmint hole was clearly a man in deep trouble, the corporal thought. They might have to shoot him. But now he himself was filled with doubt and indecision. If he left to get help, abandoning the lieutenant in such a state, he might hurt himself. Or hurt somebody. If he stayed, what good could he do? Thinking it over carefully, he judged that the best course for him to follow was retreat. Accordingly, he saluted, about faced and marched off playing, "When Johnny Comes Marching Home."

Dumbfounded, Gibson watched the solitary march of the bugler.

Shaking his head, he looked around for better help, but now the street was miraculously empty. It was chowtime at Fort Concho, and soldiers and town folks alike held to that custom. Gibson tried the door of Doc Gibbs' office. The doctor had all kinds of tools in there. He was the surgeon, the dentist, the pharmacist of Fort Concho—all these and more. The door was locked. Turning, he caught sight of the livery stable. Ah, salvation. He would find both Doodad and a tool—a saw, a hammer, something with which to pry up a couple of boards. Doodad wouldn't be much help, he told himself, loping across the street. With his shoulders hunched around his ears, Doodad looked no bigger than a glass drinking straw.

"Hah!" Gibson exclaimed. Doodad would be all things for Lovie. Doodad was the tool he needed.

Gibson plunged into the shadows of the livery stable and found Doodad sitting on a barrel and eating a pork sandwich.

"Doodad, the baby fell through the hole in Doc's porch. Come help me get her out."

Doodad tossed the sandwich over his shoulder and broke into a dead run, almost keeping up with Gibson. He slid headfirst into the hole, and soon Lovie's head appeared, followed by her shoulders. All the rest of Lovie emerged easily. Now, thank God, she was in Gibson's arms, and Doodad was squeezing himself out of a hole that seemed much smaller than the one he had dived into minutes earlier.

Lovie put her hands on Gibson's chest and pushed herself away so she could see his face. She did not like what she saw. Her lips trembled. Her chin quivered. She frowned. She stiffened her back and her legs. She made her hands into small fists. Then she opened her mouth, and the cry that came forth was a terrifying mix of outrage and sorrow and an indignation so intense that Gibson paled.

"Lovie! Good Lord!" Gibson said. "I'm really sorry. Please forgive me. I'm not accustomed to little babies like you. I've been thinking about getting married. But, now, I don't think it's a good idea. I'm not cut out to be a father." Walking back and forth in front of Doc Gibbs' office, he hummed and crooned in a voice he had never used before. "You are just about the prettiest baby I've ever been around," he hummed. "I think you're the best baby in the whole world, even with your godawful temper. Doodad, is she frequently like this?"

Doodad, gazing fondly at Lovie, simply nodded.

As Gibson walked, his spurs jangled. The heels of his boots kept the beat. He patted Lovie's back. Her screaming cries continued. Then he remembered the prize.

When Gibson was in the fourth grade back in Pennsylvania, he had won a whistling contest, and the baby goat he received as a prize caused such pride in his family that he had just kept on whistling. However, since he had been assigned to Fort Concho, he had found very little to whistle about. But here was a challenge, bigger than any fourth grade contest.

"Lovie, I'm going to whistle a tune for you," he said.

Inspired, he cleared his throat, spit, pursed his lips and began to whistle. "'Tis the Last Rose of Summer," he whistled, and the sound was not so much a whistle as a warble. It was that beautiful. By the time he got to "her lovely companions all faded and gone," Lovie stopped crying. Oh, one or two teardrops overflowed and rolled down her cheeks, but the storm was over. Lovie put her thumb in her mouth and her head on Gibson's shoulder. He breathed a sigh of relief. Forgiven. He had totally confessed and been forgiven. In love all over again with the idea of marriage, he and Lovie returned to the rocking chair.

Hearing the whirring, whirring sounds of a buggy's wheels, he looked down the street and saw Doc's buggy, pulled by a big bay mare named Molly who was high-stepping along like the purebred horse she was. The doctor pulled up sharply in front of his office and pitched a coin to Doodad. In a single motion the coin was caught and pocketed.

"Doodad, Molly's hot. Take the harness off and walk her until she cools down. Then give her a bucket of oats and rub her down."

"Sure will," Doodad said cheerfully and, taking the reins, he headed back to the livery stable.

"Lieutenant, I thought I was tired till I saw you. You look plumb wore out."

"Taking care of a cranky baby is a lot harder than most people realize."

"Has she eaten?"

"Does she eat?"

"Man, what have you fed her?"

"A bottle of, I think it was goat milk."

"She's been on cow's milk. And she enjoys a little soft food, too." Hands on his hips, the doctor stood looking down at the sleeping baby. "She looks all right to me," he said.

"Doc, she's not all right. Quint Carpenter and Bear Coltrain are on their way here right now. This is Noah's lost baby girl, and to get at Noah, they'd likely harm her. Kidnap her again or even kill her."

Doctor Tibbs said, "Everybody in town knows about this baby. I'm pretty sure of that. But nobody knows she's Noah's lost baby girl. I didn't know it myself until you told me."

"They know Miss Mary has a little colored baby. If Quint and Coltrain hear about that, they'll put it all together. We've got to hide her."

"A baby's hard to hide in a place such as this."

"Especially a colored baby with green eyes. And Lovie's got her daddy's green eyes."

"Noah's eyes. You're right. Makes it harder. Bring her on into my office and let's see if we can't puzzle this out."

Doc's office was cluttered. Looking at a desk hidden by medical books and journals, old cups of coffee, cigars and ashtrays full of cigars stubs, a couple of mousetraps, and a silver buckle, Lieutenant Gibson felt reassured. With an office as cluttered as this, Doc Tibbs would have to have an exceptional mind to be able to find anything in it.

Doc gestured toward a barrel back chair on one side of the desk. "Take a seat, Lieutenant."

Gibson sat down and rearranged the baby in his lap. Doc Tibbs unearthed a brand new leather shoelace from the clutter on the desk and gave it to Lovie to help with the teething. Next he splashed whiskey into glasses and handed one to the lieutenant. "Not on duty, are you?"

Gibson shook his head. "Baby duty," he chuckled. "Until this hit me, I was thinking about getting married."

"I passed on it, myself," Doc Tibbs said. "Now tell me all about Noah and this baby of his."

Gibson did. After he had told as much as he knew of Noah's ride, he finished by telling how Bear and Quint had set Noah's house on fire, burning up his wife and two little boys, and, apparently, kidnapping the baby. "Noah thinks the baby is most likely dead," Gibson said. "Noah's a good man," he added. "And when I sent him out of here, he rode off thinking he had nothing to lose but his life."

Awed by the tragedy of the story, the men sat in silence. The office was filled with last rays of the sun and Lovie's gurgling. Gibson eased her to the floor and the two men watched like hawks as she crawled around, first one of them taking a button or a peanut out of her mouth and then the other one retrieving a pin, a spent bullet, another peanut.

Finally, "I got an idea," Doc Tibbs said. "But there's a catch to it. I just took Mary Mills home. To her sister's place. I'm not sure Constance can take care of her, and Duff's wandered off. His aim is to get a picture of a scalping. He thinks that would put him in the history books," Doc Tibbs chuckled. "But he's most likely going to end up being the man scalped and nobody there to take a picture of it. Why, Duff is out there now, looking for Indians."

"By himself?"

"As far as Mary knows. She says Duff doesn't have a scary nerve in his body. Mary has no idea when he will return, but I told Constance to get out of that rope-broke rocking chair and take care of Mary. When I left, leastways, she was up. I'll look in on them tomorrow. Miss Mary's already fretting about Lovie, and ordinarily Lovie would be just the medicine for her. With Duff's help, they could probably manage. Barely. But they live right here, and word gets around. There are no secrets in Fort Concho. If we tell Miss Mary that Quint and Coltrain will be here any minute, she might let us hide Lovie."

"Where? Where would we hide her?"

"In plain sight," Doc Tibbs said. Grinning widely, he smoothed his mustache, curling it up at the corners.

Now Gibson was grinning. "I give up," he said. "Where are we going to hide a cranky baby?"

"As soon as it's dark, we'll take her over to Bastrop's place."

"The livery stable?"

"Yep. Lily Bastrop's got seven of her own, and one more won't be noticeable. I'll let her know that her newest youngun' is between her and the Lord."

Gibson slapped Doc Tibbs on his back. "That's the dandiest thing I ever heard. Kind of like a virgin birth."

Laughing, they clinked their glasses, took another swig of whiskey and settled down to wait for darkness to fall. Gibson picked up the baby and began to whistle a tune he was partial to. "The Yellow Rose of Texas" was the tune he warbled and, relaxed by whiskey and pure joy, he had never sounded half so good.

The Fort Concho folks walking down the wooden walkway in front of the office heard whistling the likes of which they had never heard before. One fellow thought it might be a parrot, blown in from a far off place, maybe Ethiopia, and taught to sing. Stranger things have happened. Those walking by paused, looked up searching for the bird, peered into the dark office, and then, smiling, they walked on by.

Lieutenant Gibbons continued to warble, and Doc Tibbs soon came in with the lyrics. His was a deep baritone, and he sang loudly and with vigor. So wrapped up were they in their duet, they failed to hear the sound of hoof-beats that slowed to a cautious walk and stopped in front of the livery stable.

Two riders dismounted. "Boy," one said, "take good care of these horses and there'll be an Eagle for you when we've finished our business."

"You want 'em unsaddled," Derwood asked.

The rider snorted. "Naw. The business we got here won't take long."

The man drew his gun, checked the chambers to be sure it was fully loaded and holstered it again. "Come on, Bear," he said. "Let's finish it."

* * *

The second night out of Fort Concho, Noah pitched camp in a grove of mesquite and, unable to resist the idea of hot coffee, built a small fire. He let it burn long enough to heat the coffee before he kicked it out. The ground where the fire had burned was warm, and he put his bedroll there. That night he slept better than he had slept in weeks.

The next morning he opened his eyes to a clear sky and brisk weather. Other than a rattlesnake and a scorpion, he had seen no signs of danger. The thought came that if he could spend the rest of his life alone on the plains, it would suit him. He made another fire and, lounging against his saddle, drank the hot coffee. A scissortail swooped low over his camp to perch in a mesquite tree nearby. Cocking its head to the left and the right, the bird sang a raspy, plaintive song.

Noah watched his hobbled animals contentedly grazing the new spring grasses. Nibbling the bright green sprigs, they occasionally lifted their heads to emit short, contented neighs. The dun horse that Jake Pratt had given him was sensible and strong, and Noah was becoming right fond of the gelding, even pondering on a name that would be suitable. Although the horse had technically become the property of the army when Noah enlisted, the lieutenant had acknowledged Noah's former ownership by ordering Noah to saddle the dun.

The scissortail opened its beak and emitted a long series of raspy, angry calls. It spread its wings, flew into the air, circled lower, and still lower until it pecked Noah's head. Noah threw back his head and laughed. "You got a lion's heart in that little body," he said. "And you want me gone from here. This your territory."

Noah gathered his provisions and repacked the mule. "After I name my horse, I'll settle on a name for you," he said to the mule. "Talking to a mule," he said to himself, grinning. "Well, that's better than talking to most folks." Quickly, he saddled his horse and headed the small caravan southwest. His idea was to stay in the saddle until dark.

All morning long he rode the western edge of the Texas Hill Country that was rapidly fading into the Chihuahuan Desert. For the first time in his life, he took note of the wildflowers through which he rode, enjoying the yellow of the Texas stars, the orange of the Indian paint, the blue of the bluebonnets, although he had no idea that the flowers had names. Names were facts, and it was just lately that he had become interested in facts. It was a fact that he, Noah Freeman, was riding a horse on the Texas plains. But he did not have a birthday. Most of the soldiers at the fort had birthdays, and they knew how old they were. Maybe he'd put his mind to it and think up a birthday. Maybe he could decide on his age. Satisfied, he lifted the reins and kicked the horse into a lope.

By late evening the wind was picking up and dry lightning was decorating the western sky. Both animals, lifting their heads, whinnying, wheeling suddenly, were skittish. Noah had been in the cavalry long enough to know that sometimes a horse knew more than the man riding him. He scanned the horizon ahead, but saw nothing that might offer shelter. He kept riding.

Slowly, black clouds gathered, hurrying along behind him. He put the dun into a trot, and the mule eagerly kept abreast. He caught a whiff of rain and, over his right shoulder, saw an enormous black cloud spiraling downward so that it touched the ground behind him. He put the horse into a run and, again, the mule kept abreast. Now the rain was coming in sheets, the thunder sounded like cannon, and frequent bursts of lightning lit up the sky. He soon lost all sense of direction. Realizing the storm had overtaken him, Noah put the horse into a walk. Then, not able to see as far as his saddle horn, he dropped the reins so that the dun could pick his own path.

Suddenly, the horse stopped, then wheeled around so fast and with such strength that the mule's lead rope slid from around saddle horn and slid through his hand, rope-burning the hand. The mule gave a long, high cry of terror, and bucking and kicking up its heels, disappeared into the rain and the wind as Noah watched helplessly.

Holding the horse's reins firmly, he dismounted and, using the horse for shelter, poor as the shelter was, he knew he had to wait out the storm. The rain died to a sorry drizzle and the wind stopped. But not a star hung in the sky nor a sliver of the moon. Nothing left but to make the best of where he was until the light came on. He hobbled the dun and unsaddled him. He sat on the cold, wet ground, put his head on the saddle and, somehow, slept, now and then waking to the horse's gentle nudging.

When he felt daylight on his eyes, he opened them. He got to his feet, took a few steps and peed. Soundlessly. It was a full minute before he looked down and saw that he was peeing into a canyon. "Praise the Lord," he said. "If it hadn't been for my horse, all three of us would have tumbled down that canyon wall."

The wall of the canyon was not steep. To Noah it was a canyon, but it was hardly a canyon at all, but a draw that ran water only when it rained. It wasn't deep. He saw a pond down below, a small pond, but with the fresh rain, fine enough to satisfy a horse. In the daylight, they could make their way down. Easy.

He threw the saddle on the horse, cinched it up, and the two made their way down into the canyon. The horse headed to the pond and drank noisily and slowly, snorting and tossing his head with the pure pleasure of drinking. Noah heard the braying of the mule and looking up, saw that it was slowly coming up the draw toward him.

"Well, now, looky here, things is looking up. Sho is now."

He would gladly have chanced a fire for hot coffee, but everything was soaked. He put some coffee in a cup, filled it with water, and set it in the sun to seep. "Better'n nothin'," he told himself.

He went down to the pond to wash up. Leaning over, he saw his face in the water and fell back on his heels. "Well, now, let's just see about this," he muttered. He leaned over the pond again and again saw the wavery image of a cavalry soldier. Soldier. "Glory be," he said. "That ain't nobody in the world but me. Noah Freeman." He looked again and saw a colored soldier, as big as any man.

He'd have to sit awhile and ponder this—scared by his own self. He'd seen plenty of colored soldiers, but he'd never seen his own self lately. In fact, he had only seen his own self two or three times. But all this time he had been seeing himself at Massa Ellerbee's, seeing hisself like he was then.

On the plantation, one of his jobs was ice. He would cut up ice on the lake in the winter, wrap it in tow sacks and bury it. When summer came he would dig it up for the white folks. When he would haul it up there, he would usually leave it on the back porch. There was a mirror there and he'd look at himself, seeing himself in rags, turning to see his back scarred by the whip, shoulders hunched, head down. But here he was, on the plains of Texas, a soldier. He wasn't a darky slave. He was a soldier. He stayed by the pond all day, thinking it through. His reflection disappeared, but it stayed on his mind.

The next morning he drank hot coffee, repacked the mule, and got on his horse, turning once more toward Fort Stockton. He thought of all the folks who had sent him away, hidden him, given him a horse to run away on. Most of these folks had gotten in bad trouble. Jake was dead, and

Uncle Daniel was sorely treated. Now Lieutenant Gibson had sent him running again.

When he figured it was about noontime, he found shade under a tree near a dry creek bed, dismounted, and took a long pleasurable drink. The dun nudged his shoulders. He turned and looked at him and, looking, a name came. "Jericho. Your name is Jericho. And you most likely the only horse in Texas named after a battle. And Jericho, we're going back to Fort Concho. I done left off running from Quint and his kind."

With that pronouncement, he turned Jericho around and headed the caravan toward the northeast. As he rode, Noah talked to himself and to his horse.

"Jericho, I'm giving my own self a fact," he said. "My birthday is gonna be May the first. And another fact: I'm twenty-eight this here year. Next year I'll be twenty-nine. Then thirty. And Jericho, don't you forget it." Jericho flickered his ears and lifted his tail in reply.

Enjoying the wildflowers that had appeared over night, Noah's brain suddenly flipped. "Whoa," he said, realizing it had flipped onto something like a miracle fact. Bear Coltrain and Quint were looking for a nigger slave! They were not looking for him, not looking for this soldier, this man riding a war horse and with a gun he could shoot and in the company of a provisioned mule. This might be his last ride, and he would make it a damn fine ride. What did he have to lose? He set his hat at an angle, straightened his shoulders and sat tall in the saddle. Then he spurred Jericho toward Fort Concho.

Chapter Ten

by Jim Lee

Noah turned back east and started the long trek back toward Fort Concho. But before he had gone a mile, he began to worry about what would happen to him if he failed to carry out the order Lieutenant Gibson had given him. If he went back, he would be disobeying orders. He could be court martialed, and, what was worse in his mind, he could get Lieutenant Gibson in trouble. So Noah turned Jericho and his pack mule west again. He looked at the map Lieutenant Gibson had drawn for him. When he left Angelo, he was told to follow the Middle Concho River west till he reached the headwaters, and then Lieutenant Gibson said, "It gets a little tricky."

He laid the map down and showed Noah how it would be between the headwaters and the Pecos. He said, "Here is what you do, Noah. You wait there at the headwaters till you see a wagon train or the Butterfield Stage or a bunch of pilgrims heading west, and then you join up with them."

"What if they ain't no train going west, sir?"

"Well, that depends on whether there has been any rain. If it has rained, you follow the ruts in the trail and you will come to a series of ponds that should have water in them. Here they are marked on a map drawn in 1849 by a lieutenant named Bryan. The first one you will see is called Mustang Ponds, then Flat Rock Ponds, and then Wild China Ponds."

"Yessir, I see 'em."

"Now after you leave Wild China Ponds, you have got thirty or forty miles till you see a gap in the Castle Mountains. It is marked here as Castle Gap, and it's not too far from there to the Pecos and Horsehead Crossing. See it?"

"Yes, sir, I see the gap. And how far from there to the Pecos River?"

"About ten miles over some rough country. And the damned Pecos can be tricky to cross. Old Charlie Goodnight and his herd made it through four or five years ago and named this stretch the Goodnight-Loving Trail. It is littered with dead cattle and horses, so you have to be careful."

"Oh, I will. You don't know how many rivers I have crossed between here and the Mississipi," Noah said.

"Yeah, Noah, but you have never crossed one in the desert where rivers can dry up or run wild, and the Pecos has been called a graveyard."

So now Noah figured that after all that hellacious rain he had suffered through a few nights ago, he should at least have water on the seventy-five miles or so from the headwaters of the Middle Concho to the Pecos. Then things would take care of themselves. Maybe.

Noah camped along the Middle Concho, made a fire, and boiled some beans and a little bacon to go with his hardtack. While the beans cooked he hobbled the horse and the mule in some good grass along the river. After supper and two cups of strong coffee, Noah put out the fire, rolled out his bedroll, and slept the sleep of the tired and innocent till daylight woke him. After more coffee and a couple of rashers of dry bacon from the provisions in his pack, he saddled Jericho, loaded the heavy pack on the mule, and set out west again. The pack was heavy because, in addition to his supplies, Noah was taking several hundred rounds of ammunition for the new breach-loading carbines the army was using along the Indian frontier. Lieutenant Gibson told Noah the men in the frontier forts could always use more rounds. When the Middle Concho played out, Noah saw the trail the cattlemen and stage drivers and wagon trains had worn in the western edge of the Hill Country and eastern part of the Chihuahuan Desert, though he didn't know either name. He just knew to head west toward the three ponds on the map and the gap in the mountains. Maybe he could make it to Fort Stockton in a week or two.

Nobody had told Noah that this part of the Chihuahuan Desert was the Comanche War Trail, the route the Comanches took on their raids into Mexico. Noah had ridden for five days when he saw the Castle Mountains off in the distance. And in another day, he was close enough to see the gap. It was then that he heard the first gunshots. They were a couple of miles off, so Noah dismounted, led his horse and mule into a draw and hunkered down to see who was doing all the shooting. He didn't see any Indians, but it wasn't long till he saw an army patrol rushing toward his hiding place. Noah could make out no more than twenty or so cavalry troopers riding hard in his direction. He jumped up and waved his hat at them and then tethered his horse to a tree root sticking out into the draw. He led the mule farther down the gulch till he found another root growing out of the dry creek bed.

By the time Noah was back up on the edge of the draw, the troopers were coming to a stop and dismounting. A major came toward Noah and said, "Report."

"Well, sir, I am Private Noah Freeman and I was sent west to Fort Stockton by Lieutenant Gibson."

"He sent you deep into Indian country all by yourself? Why? Are you a courier with an important message?"

"Sir, I don't know what a 'courier' is and I ain't got no message. I just got some provisions and several hundred rounds of ammunition for y'all's rifles on that pack mule over yonder."

The major called out, "Sergeant, come take care of this man. Then get the troopers lined up along this bank to repel the Indians that are regrouping and will be here before you can say 'lock and load.'"

"Yessir! Now, soldier, who the hell are you? Can you shoot that rifle you have in your horse's scabbard and that Navy Colt in your holster? And what the hell are you doing out all by yourself? Are you a deserter? Are you crazy enough to be in Indian country all alone?"

"I can't answer all them questions at one time, sir," Noah said.

"Don't call me sir. I am a sergeant. Didn't they teach you anything when you became a trooper?"

"Well, sergeant, Lieutenant Gibson from Fort Concho sent me out here because they was some men tryin' to kill me—"

"All right, all right! Just get your gun and line up with them other soldiers along the bank. We'll see soon enough if you can handle that gun you're holding. Them damned redskins will be topping that rise between here and Castle Mountain over yonder in about ten minutes. If we're lucky."

The sergeant went down the line where the troops' horses were being held by three or four soldiers. They ran a rope through the bridles and tied the horses to a tree farther down the draw.

"I want two of you men to stay with the horses no matter what. You others come with me."

Noah fell in alongside the soldiers lining the edge of the draw with rifles loaded and ready. He asked the man next to him, "What are y'all doin' out here runnin' away from some Indians I don't see."

"You'll see 'em soon enough. We was escorting that major you see back to Concho. He was out at Stockton on an inspection tour for Phil Sheridan. We was seeing him safely home when we got jumped by a Comanche war party heading south into Mexico. At least I guess that's where they were going. Maybe they was just out to count a little coup and take a few white scalps. Musta been a hundred of 'em. They started shooting and we started runnin' to see if we could find someplace to make a stand. The lieutenant who was leading our patrol and three or four troopers got killed, but we couldn't wait to bury them. If we can stand off these Indians, we can go back and give 'em a Christian burial. If not, I guess the buzzards and the coyotes will get them. This whole damn desert is loaded with bones of men and animals."

"Damn," Noah said, "I should have stayed at Saint Angela and faced old Quint and Bear Coltrain."

The soldier next to Noah said, "We was hoping to run into a patrol coming west, but all we found was one lone colored soldier—the first one I ever seen. Maybe them redskins will want a black scalp to hang on some brave's belt."

He thought that was funny and laughed.

Noah said, "Shit, man, I better see if the shootin' I learned at Fort Concho will work way out here in this damned desert. Then maybe I can save this scalp—and yours too."

"You ain't jokin' about that. Your wooly head may depend on it."

Noah asked, "What kind of Indians are y'all runnin' from? Them Kiowas I heard about?"

"Hell no. Them is Comanche. Or maybe Apaches. I think Comanches, but you are gonna know soon enough. There may be a hundred of 'em.

They are a mile or two behind us," the soldier said, "and they are madder than hell."

"How come?" Noah said.

"'Cause they jumped us just as we came through the gap, and we managed to kill about fifteen of them devils. Say, what the hell are you doing out here on the Comanche War Trail by yourself?"

"I didn't know it was no war trail. My lieutenant sent me to Fort Stockton to join up with some troops out there and take 'em that ammunition I got on that pack mule."

"The major'll be damned glad to get the extra rounds. That was the major that spotted you first. Here he comes now."

As Noah and the soldier were talking, the short, stocky major came down the line of men looking to see how many had been shot in the skirmish with the Indians. Four or five of the men were being bandaged up and one or two were laid out on the ground looking near death.

The major called the soldiers to him and said, "Men, this looks like a good place to make a stand. There is not much cover except for the bank of this draw, but we can see the Indians as they come over that rise, and they will be on horseback. Being holed up here will give us some advantage. I don't want another damned running fight with that war party even though we made out a little better than they did. I counted about ten or fifteen of them on the ground. What did you get, Sergeant?"

"Looks like about that many. What was all them horses they was herding all about?"

"I imagine they were stolen off Mexican ranches and they were taking that remuda back north. Maybe they won't be as eager to fight us if think they can get off with all those horses."

Noah looked around him and saw that the soldiers were all white, and for the first time it seemed to register on the major that there was a Negro soldier now in the ranks of the company he was leading. "Who are you, soldier?" he asked Noah.

Noah was on his feet with his hat squared on his head as he jumped to salute the major. "I am Noah Freeman, sir."

"Yeah, that's what you said earlier, But what are you doing out here in this damned desert all by yourself?"

"Yessir, I was sent out here by Lieutenant Gibson to make it to Fort Stockton to report to the garrison there. He told me to take some bullets for your repeater rifles and report for duty at the fort."

"And the damned fool didn't know better than to send you into Indian country by yourself. And you didn't have any better sense than to go?"

"Well, sir, they was some mens layin' off to kill me in Angela, and the lieutenant thought I would be safer out west. I didn't know about no Indians. I mean, I knowed there was Indians in this country, but I ain't never seen one. I ain't been in the army out here all that long."

"You ever shoot anybody?" the major asked.

"Well, sir, I joined up with some Union soldiers after I got out of Mississippi, and we shot at a lot of Rebs as we moved west. But I don't know if I ever hit one."

"Were you in the army then?"

"No sir, I was with Captain John Malone and his men for awhile before I managed to make it to Texas. I didn't join the army till I got to Fort Worth after the war was done over. I thought I might as well draw thirteen dollars a month as starve trying to farm and ranch over in Tarrant County. My family was all dead, so I decided to enlist."

"All, right, report to that sergeant you were talking to and he will tell you where to line up when the Comanches come."

"Yes sir," Noah said and saluted.

The major returned the salute and went along the line to see to his men.

It was getting late in the afternoon when Noah saw a cloud of dust rising in the west. He called out, "Look over yonder, sergeant! I think I see some Indians slowly moving this way. At least they are men on horses. I 'spect they is Indians."

The major saw the horsemen riding toward them and called the troops to attention. "Men, I think the Indians are coming this way. Get down low and let's see if we can surprise them. They may expect us to still be on horseback."

The Indians came slowly. There was one loping ahead of the others looking down at the ground for sign. In a minute, he raised rifle above his head and shouted something that the soldiers could barely hear.

Then the Indians started running toward the draw where the soldiers lay in wait. The major hollered down the line, "Hold your fire, men! Don't shoot till you see me pull the trigger. Then try to aim at the horse's belly. You probably can't hit an Indian on horseback at this distance, but if you down the horse, you will have some damned savage afoot."

Noah turned to the man next to him and said, "Man, I surely do hate to shoot at a horse. I had rather try to down an Indian without killing a pore innocent horse."

The soldier, a veteran of Shiloh and Vicksburg named McCorqual, said, "You better do what the major says. Them damned Rebs didn't think twice about killing our horses back during the war. A man without a horse is an easier target."

As the Indians came toward the draw at full tilt, the major stood up, aimed his carbine at the lead horse, and screamed, "Fire! Fire!"

The horse fell as the soldiers all opened fire at once. Three or four horses went down, and the Indians who were dismounted fell behind the oncoming horsemen.

Noah Freeman, a man who hated to kill anything, especially a good piece of horseflesh, took careful aim at an Indian off to the right of the pack and fired. The Indian fell, and Noah chambered another round and fired again. This time he missed, and McCorqual said, "Goddamit, nigger, I told you to shoot at the horses not the Indians!"

Noah said, "The first time I got an Indian, and I thought—"

"You are a soldier, and you ain't paid to think. Do what you are told."

With three or four horses down and at least one Indian—Noah's—lying motionless on the ground, the Comanche war party fell back out of rifle range. They didn't go far, but circled around a stand of cactus and seemed to be arguing.

Noah said to McCorqual, "How come them Indians got all them repeater rifles? I thought they used bows and arrows and clubs and sticks and such."

"Don't worry, they got clubs and sticks and arrows too, but some of them have rifles they have either taken off dead soldiers or traded for from the Comancheros."

"The what?"

"Comancheros are white men and Mexicans who trade with the

Comanches and the Apaches and other Indians out here. The army tries to run them off, but they sneak in and trade with the Indians. They bring in guns and trade for Mexican girls and captured white girls and gold and stuff, I guess."

While Noah was getting this lesson in life on the Texas plains, the Indians turned again and came toward the draw with screams and shouts and guns blazing. This time they spread out and made harder targets. The soldiers by now were out of the draw firing as the Indians closed fast. McCorqual fell dead beside Noah, and three or four other soldiers were hit and fell back into the gulch. The soldiers kept firing and the Indians keep coming.

Noah had slipped down beside McCorqual to see if he was really dead when an Indian rode over him into the draw waving what looked like a hatchet at one of the soldiers who was hit. Noah jerked out the Navy Colt he had never fired and shot the Indian through the back of the head just as he was about to hack the soldier to death. Before Noah had time to think, three other Indians rode down into the gulch holding spears and war clubs. Noah shot one in the heart and ducked away from the one who had a hatchet raised to kill him.

Noah dropped his gun when he ducked away from the Indian, but he picked up a rock about as big as a cantaloupe and threw it right into the Indian's face. The Indian cried out and fell and Noah jumped on him and snapped his neck with one quick jerk of his hands.

As the other Indian turned toward Noah, the major shot him in the middle of the chest. As the Indian fell, the major took an arrow—the first one Noah had ever seen—in his right shoulder. He screamed in pain, but Noah had no time to help him because Indians were coming into the open end of the draw firing rifles and shooting arrows and slashing with hatchets. They were on horseback, but the soldiers managed to kill most of them with pistols and rifles and one with a saber he had taken from the lieutenant who came in wounded and was now dead.

Suddenly it was all over. The Indians who didn't die in the gulch rode out to join the seven or eight who stayed up on the plain above the draw. As the soldiers fired a few shots at the retreating Indians, the Comanches rode hard away from the scene of the battle.

"Reckon they had all they can stand?" Noah asked one of the men who had survived the onslaught.

"Damn if I know. Them goddam savages ain't like white folks. They might do anything. Oh, 'scuse me, I mean they ain't like whites or coloreds. I will say this for the colored soldiers I served with at Chicamauga and Pea Ridge, they fought like devils out of hell. And so do you, soldier."

The major lay in the ditch with the arrow sticking out of his shoulder as Noah and the other soldier, a private named Nash, looked around to see who was dead and who was alive. The major said to Noah, "Freeman, you fought better than most white soldiers I ever commanded. I thank you for saving me. Now quit gawking and pull this goddam arrow out."

Noah looked at Nash and then back at the major, "Sir, I don't know as I can pull that thing out. Don't arrows have a barb on the end like a fish-hook? I don't see that hook, sir."

"Of course you don't see the damned arrowhead—that is what the goddam thing is called—because it is stuck inside my body. Now you and Nash there get it out! Get the goddam thing out! Now!"

Noah thought, I ain't no damn doctor, but I guess I better think what to do. Noah turned the major part way over and ripped the back of his shirt off. He told Nash, "O.K. man, grab that arrow and push it plum through and out this side."

Nash said, "Push it through? What the hell do you mean 'push it through'? Are you crazy?"

"Shit, man," Noah said, "It's gonna be a whole lot worse if we just jerk it out backwards. Now I am gonna hold the major still and when I count to three, I want you to push the hell out of that thing. Get it in one whack!"

The major, who had half passed out, said, "He is right, soldier, you have to push it out and then cut the head off that thing. Then Freeman here can pull it out."

Noah held the major steady and counted to three. Nash turned white, but he pushed like hell and the arrow head came out the major's back. The major made no sound, and then Noah saw that he was either passed out or dead. Noah reached around the man's back and broke off the arrowhead. Then he pulled hard and the arrow came out with a small gush of blood. Noah said to Nash, "Ain't they no doc in this troop to see after the major, to see if he is dead?"

"Yeah," Nash said, "there he is lying right over yonder with a bullet right between his eyes. Looks to me like you the doctor now, boy."

"You know, I wish you wouldn't call me 'boy.' That is what old Massa Ellerbee back on the plantation used to call men as old as sixty, though Lord knows not many of them lived that long. I think I have done a man's work here today."

"Soldier—what is your real name?"

"It's Freeman, Noah Freeman."

"Well, Noah Freeman, you are goddam' sure a man if I ever saw one. I would go into battle with you anytime the army has got somebody to fight."

"I appreciate that, Private Nash. Now let's see how many of us is still alive and see whether there is enough of us left to fight when them Indians gather up and come back."

Nash said, "Nah, they ain't comin' back. We killed their war chief and way too many of their braves. Some of 'em may come back in the night to take up their dead if they can find them. What we got to do is bury our dead before we skedaddle out of here to Concho."

The major began to moan. One of the men who had the medic's bag got out a bottle of whiskey and brought it to the major. He said, "Major, we gonna give you a short drank of this here whiskey and then we gonna pour a little of it in that wound you got."

The soldier gave the major a drink and then poured about two ounces of whiskey into the front of the major's wound and about an ounce into the side where the arrow came out. The major gritted his teeth but made no sound. Noah thought, that major is surely enough a man if I ever seen one.

There were seven men left who were able to fight if it came to that. Eight were wounded and might be able to either ride or be dragged on some kind of makeshift travois back to Concho. The major told the soldier who had the best horse to ride as fast as he could back to Concho and get as many wagons as he could find and meet them along the trail. He said if they met an immigrant train to commandeer their wagons to take the wounded back to Concho. It was closer to Fort Stockton, but the chances of running into the remnant of that war party or some other band of Indians was greater going west than going east.

The major called Noah to him and said, "I saw what you did when those Indians rushed us. I saw how many you killed. I even saw you disobey my order and shoot that first Indian instead of shooting his horse. I don't give a good goddam' what color you are or how long you have been in the army, I am making you acting sergeant. Now I want you to organize these men and start burying our dead."

"Sir, I don't know nothing about—"

"Just get to it, Sergeant!"

The major called the men to him and told them what he had done. He said, "When Sergeant Freeman says 'jump' you damned dog soldiers better jump."

Noah found some trenching tools on one of the mules the troop had been using for pack animals and set about digging graves for the men who had been killed. When the graves had been dug and the bodies laid out beside them, Noah went back to the major and asked, "Sir, do we have anybody here who can read some Scripture or say a few words over the men we 'bout to bury out here in this lonesome place?"

The major said, "Is Private Jackson still alive?"

"I don't know, sir. What he look like?"

"He is an older man, maybe fifty years old, and he has a gray moustache."

Noah said, "No, sir, that man died in the first bunch of Indians that come over the ditch, but he took three Indians with him. I saw him as I was gettin' up from hittin' that Indian with a rock. I saw that old man shoot one and knife one and then cut one's throat. He was some kind of tough."

"All right, Acting Sergeant, when you make a list of names of the men killed, I want you to put Private Jackson's name down, and then I want you to write his real name. You can write can't you?

"Well, sort of, sir. Captain Malone taught me to read. I can read readin', but I can't read writing."

"You mean handwriting?"

"Yessir."

"All right, Sergeant, get one of the men that can write writin' and have him write beside Jackson's name, the name of General James F. J. Johnston. That is who he really was. He didn't know I knew him, but he was a brigadier general in the Confederate Army. I fought against him at the Cumberland Gap when he was just a major and again in The Wilderness when he was a general. He was as good an officer as Lee had in his army there at the end of the war."

"Sir, if he was a general, how come he is a private in the U. S. Cavalry now?"

"I can't answer that. Maybe his family was all dead and the army was all he knew. He was a damned good general and a fine private. I never fought against a man I admired more."

Noah was puzzled, "Sir, how could a general get busted down so low?"

"Hell, Sergeant, I was a major general at the end of the war. But it was a temporary rank, and if I wanted to stay in the army, I had to go back to the rank I had when the war started."

"Should I call you general, sir?"

"No, a man is what he is paid, and I am paid as a major of cavalry. Now go and make up the lists and get the bodies buried. Maybe somebody has a Bible and can say some words over the men who didn't make it."

When Noah and the men had buried all the bodies and hauled rocks from the dry river bed to pile on the graves to keep the coyotes out, Noah asked Nash, "What we gonna do with all them dead Indians? The major didn't say nothing about what to do with them."

"We are gonna let them rot out here on this damned desert unless the other Indians come back and drag them off. I don't care if the buzzards peck the eyes out of ever' one of them bastards. Maybe we had better drag the dead ones down here in this gulch and put 'em up there with the ones we killed before they jumped down into this ditch."

That night, Noah heard sounds out on the prairie. He and the other men splayed out along the bank and watched as a dozen or more Indians crept out and began dragging their dead back toward Castle Gap. One soldier wanted to pick off as many Indians as he could, but the major, who had been going in and out of consciousness, told Noah to have the men stand down.

The major said, "No, Sergeant, keep the men quiet. The Indians care as much about their dead as we do, and with that many dead, they don't have enough braves to attack us again. They will take their dead home and wait till another day to kill U.S. Cavalry."

Noah posted a watch and let half the men sleep while the others kept a lookout. Nobody seemed to mind taking orders from a colored soldier, especially after the major put him in charge and after they had seen what he could do in a fight.

Two days later, Noah had the horses all rounded up and was about ready to try to get the wounded men headed back to Concho as best he could. They had made some travois out of poles that grew along the creek bed and stretched out horse blankets. Noah told the major they would have to move since they were out of food. The major, who was now feverish but not out of his head, agreed.

Before Noah had a chance to get the wounded on the travois, he saw two wagons coming toward them from the direction of Saint Angela. They were big covered wagons, and sitting in the seats of the first one was a soldier and a woman. In the second wagon, both drivers were women.

"Whoa," one of the drivers said, "Are you men the ones we are to take back to Concho?"

"That's right," Noah said, "and you didn't come one minute too soon. I was about to start dragging these wounded men back to the fort on these here dragging stretchers, and I doubt that a one of them would have made it five miles."

"And who the hell are you, nigger boy?"

"Private, I am Acting Sergeant Noah Freeman, and I have been put in charge of this here detachment by General Walter F. Winslow hisself. He is that man you see over yonder on that stretcher. If you don't like who is in charge here, maybe you had better talk to the general."

Once Noah had learned who the major had been, he thought of him and always, for the rest of his life, spoke of him as "The General."

The wagons had plenty of water in barrels, and the women had cooked up stew the night before they reached the troops. All Noah and his men had to do was build a fire and set up the tripods the women had brought along to hold the cooking pots. In less than an hour, the soldiers were eating better than they had in years. Stew with real meat—cow meat—potatoes, and carrots, and onions. It was a feast most had not seen since before the Civil War.

When the casualties were loaded on the wagons and the men were mounted and ready to head east, Nash asked the soldier who had come out with the wagons, "Who are them women and what are they doing out here in Indian country?"

"They are what you call Quakers. They had come out in five wagons to try to civilize the Indians or something. They had some men with them when they started out, but they got killed along the way by Indians."

Nash said, "So I guess they were turning back when you took over their wagons?"

"Hell, no. They were going to go it alone and pray to the Lord that the Indians would see the way to peace. Of course they would have been killed or made into squaws before they got to Castle Gap. Hell, they may still go after we get these men back to Concho."

Noah rode in front of the few men left and out ahead of the wagons as befitted an acting non-commissioned officer. He knew that when he got back to Fort Concho, he would be back to being a private again. He also knew he would have to face up to the men who wanted him dead. But Noah Freeman had seen lots of men die in the last week, and he was sure he could hold his own against anybody now—red, white, or colored.

Chapter Eleven

by Carole Nelson Douglas

The sound of horses nickering always filled the Saint Angela livery stable. Now a baby's ceaseless bawling rang down the stalls, making the horses shuffle their shod hooves on the straw-strewn dirt floor.

The Buck brothers worked at the stable when Fort Concho had no jobs for them. So Doodad had been as happy as a bear in honey when the little colored baby was brought to Lily Bastrop to tend as one of her many own.

Now he paced in the tack room, rocking and crooning a red-faced Lovie.

"She was jest fine the first few hours," he told his brother, Derwood. "Now there's nothin' I can do to make her the happy little baby she was."

Derwood frowned. "Changing the baby rags?"

"Miz Bastrop just did all that. She can't do a thing either."

Derwood looked through the open door past the stall area into the street beyond, then scratched his neck.

"I don't know what Doc Tibbs and the lieutenant were thinkin', hiding that baby here at the livery stable. Bear Coltrain and Quint Carpenter come and go here every day, making little jaunts around the area lookin' for their 'green-eyed nigger' and Miz Mills' green-eyed baby. If this howling keeps up, they're gonna find her right fast."

"Miz Bastrop says I always cheer this baby up, but not this time."

Derwood shook his head. He'd just glimpsed a horseman pass by, and for a nasty second it had looked like Bear Coltrain.

"I know you like jiggling that baby on your knee better than anything, Doodad, but it's plain missing the one who's mothered it. You can't hide a baby like a sack of flour. You're gonna take it back to Miz Mills' adobe house outside of town."

"But the lieutenant—"

"We ain't under his command and this just ain't working." Derwood went to a big wooden box built against one tack room wall and pulled out a shotgun. As he loaded it, he said, "You take the wagon, and the baby, and this gun out to Miz Mills' place. You leave the baby and the gun with her, but first you cock both triggers, so it's ready to go if she needs it. Got that?"

"I got that, Derwood. I'm good with guns as well as babies."

Derwood grinned. A job always made Doodad feel needed, and he'd made sure his brother understood guns, when to touch them and when not to. "You don't cock those triggers until you are in Miz Mills' sister's house and that baby is in Mary Mills' arms and there is a safe place to put it, you hear?"

"I hear you, Derwood. Maybe the ride will calm the baby."

Derwood glanced at the screwed up, howling, deeply red face. He wondered if a baby could scream itself to death. No telling. "You be quick about it. I'll tell the lieutenant what we done when I see him next. And keep an eye peeled for those two bad hombres." He glanced out into the street again, worried.

* * *

Doodad did just as his brother had said, like he always did.

He didn't see a soul until the end of the trip. The ride was rough and the baby squalled through all of it, no matter how he cradled it in one arm and sang or whistled.

Mary Mills heard the horse and rig coming and was waiting outside her door, leaning lightly on a cane. When she saw what Doodad carried, she left the cane against the adobe wall and came to meet him, arms out held.

"Avril. Avril Hope. How I've missed you! My, you've been crying up a whole rainstorm."

The baby interrupted her howling to heed a familiar voice. Mary smiled and rocked her. She howled again. Stopped. Howled. Stopped. Mary crooned and tickled the reddened dusky face and then Doodad witnessed the most angelic smile he had ever seen come over those tiny features. He grinned too. The baby was quiet. He and Derwood had done the right thing.

He went back to the wagon to fetch the shotgun, then followed woman and child into the house's front room. It was a fine place, with more furniture than Doodad had seen in his life. He didn't see Miz Mills' crazy sister anywhere.

"My brother Derwood says you need to put this shotgun somewhere safe, but close at hand, in case anybody up to evil comes around."

The woman looked up from making a silly face for the gurgling infant. Her features turned stern. "Behind the tall case clock would be the best place."

Doodad cocked one trigger, then the other, and leaned the rifle gently against the wall behind the clock.

"It's ready to shoot, if you need it, ma'am. And we'll be out to check on you, and watchin' Coltrain and Carpenter."

* * *

Bear Coltrain took a swig of whiskey. That evening the Cactus Saloon was crowded with liquored-up cowboys so no one could overhear them at the moment. There wasn't much to hear but ole Quint in his cups about how that green-eyed nigger clan must be Satan's own spawn.

"That black bastard Noah was givin' me trouble back on Mr. Ellerbee's plantation," he said. "Always runnin' away, no matter how much I beat him when I caught him, or no matter how long Goliath laid the whip on him when we got 'im back and pole-tied. Never could kill 'im. Was a 'two-thou-sand-dollar' slave, they said. Spawned off some massa who took his prongin' of them negresses too serious, I bet. Old Man Ellerbee musta had a grudge against the white man who fathered that big black boy and gave him those green eyes. He said never to kill 'im and he sure wasn't gonna sell him.

"Then that ugly green-eyed black bitch sister of his that my son Ben sold around everywhere hadda go and stick Ben like a fatback hog. We took care of her good."

"And the wife and kids," Bear added. He'd gotten liquored up and got in on burning down the cabin that Noah had built, with his family still inside.

Quint's one milky eye gleamed with the memory, but it was a passing pleasure. His fist hit the table. "But he got away. That Noah! That green-eyed clan are Satan's own spawn, I tell you. Even that Noah baby we dropped in the prairie grass for the coyotes to eat ended up gettin' found and carted around town by a crazy white woman like some pickaninny princess. I'm not leavin' Saint Angela without killing that Noah bastard."

Bear Coltrain hushed Quint's rising voice. "We gotta do it legal. You're a sheriff. Take him into custody for some old charge. Who's to say what happens if he tries to escape and gets shot? He sure has a history of runnin'."

"He's gonna be beat dead. You kin shoot 'im after."

Bear nodded. Noah, who now called himself Freeman, still had claims on that sweet grazing land he and Quint had burned him out of. A dead nigger, like a dead Indian, couldn't claim anything but six feet of dirt, if anyone cared enough to bury 'im. There was a lot of opportunity for a white man in the West, but the colored and redskins shouldn't be in the runnin' for any of it, being naturally so inferior.

Bear Coltrain pondered for a moment. Quint was so full of hate it rode him the way a burr under a saddle blanket spurred a mustang to buck. Didn't make for smart thinking or moves. "Say, Quint," he drawled. "I'm figuring we been going about this the wrong way. What we want right now isn't old Noah. It's that green-eyed baby of his."

"Don't want no colored 'cept for target practice."

"The whole town's gettin' to know about that green-eyed baby, but Noah's been gone. He come back, and we have it, we got a whole lotta somethin' to deal with. That Mills woman lives in an adobe place outside of town. We could mosey over there tomorrow. You're a sheriff. You got authority."

Quint looked up from the dark-piss depths of his whiskey. The crazy milk-glass eye was gleaming again. "Yeah. Yeah! Never should have left it off, 'cause we got ole Noah by the short hairs as long as we got it. Let's go get us that baby back."

* * *

Constance Johnson was a like a seaman's wife, sitting at the window all day waiting for her roaming husband to get home. But her sea was the endless rolling waves of empty land, mesquite, and cactus scrubland. Every afternoon she'd sit in an old rope-repaired rocking chair on the scorching west side of her house, facing the sun. Her husband had left, driving cattle to California to sell, not sailing a ship to faraway ports in the China Sea.

California might be just as far, for all she knew of it.

Mary Mills sat beside her sister, rocking little Avril Hope Mills, hugging the child to her heart. Sometimes she found herself spellbound by the endless vistas of grass under the big morning-glory blue Texas sky, but she was an Ohio girl from the industrial and industrious—and enlightened—East. It disheartened her how a baby with such bright green eyes in a velvety brown face could be spurned by some. Too many southerners here. Too many rough, ignorant men on the edge of civilization who were more acquainted with whores than proper women. Mary was almost ready to leave for Ohio with her new daughter. She'd been housebound with an injury from a fall, but she hardly needed her cane any longer and could travel soon. Her sister, Constance, was sadly disturbed of mind, but Avril needed Mary more. Mary had left Cincinnati a widow with only a stillborn baby to show for married life. She'd return a mother.

Avril gurgled and stirred in her arms. Mary straightened the yellow neck frill on the baby's gown, in case it was irritating that adorable double chin. What a little sunflower she was!

As sweet-dispositioned as you could wish. She smiled to recall Derwood and his brother Doodad. Pretty uncivilized men, but that Doodad adored little Avril like a child with his own personal puppy. And Derwood truly cared for his slightly simple brother. There were good men out here, including Duff McNamara, the photographer who'd transported her goods here. But Mary wasn't of a mind to take another husband.

She just wanted a baby. This baby, that God had left sitting near a pecan tree by the road. A baby with her name on it. The color of the child's skin was no matter. Mary's father and she herself had worked in the Underground Railroad to help black slaves escape the South. This was one more soul to save from indenture. She could give this child the upbringing and education that would make her the equal of any woman of any color in the world.

So Mary rocked the baby beside her sister, crooning while Constance's lips moved silently in some mad litany of her own. Mary heard the front door of the cabin open and boot heels thump on the plain wooden floor, spurs jingling like coins. Mary detested spurs and whips being used on horses. It was so brutal.

She grabbed her cane, stood, and turned, Avril in her arms. Duff would never enter so rudely. Before she could pass through the bedroom to the front room, two large looming men filled the house with their brimmed hats and hulking forms.

"Bear Coltrain, ma'am," said one, doffing his hat.

"I've heard of you," she said. Nothing good, but she didn't say that.

"Your sister here?" he asked, looking around.

"Of course she's here. This is her house." And mine, her tone implied.The man pointed with his dusty hat, making Mary turn Avril away from the motes that floated in a sunbeam from the front room's window. "That baby yourn?"

"None of your business." During all this the other man had remained planted in place, glancing around with cold eyes, like he could level the place and everyone in it. He wore a vest with a metal star on one side. He was a sheriff up in North Texas, she'd heard. Quint Carpenter. Mary's blood chilled. She knew a merciless killer when she saw one. Many of the southern slave catchers would slay a Negro man, woman, or child like another man would smash a fly.

"'Fraid it is, ma'am." Bear Coltrain knew how to doff his hat but he was another kind of snake. A sidewinder. "There's this colored man in town, Noah, a soldier. Been a slave, I hear. Anyway, he's got green eyes jest like that baby you're holdin' there. Can't be that many green-eyed niggers in the world. That baby's likely his. We gotta take it into custody."

"In custody? An infant? If there is some claim—" Mary's heart clenched and her soul screamed No! "If there is some possibility, a judge will have to decide."

"We ain't got a judge in Saint Angela," the other man said with a smirk. "You jest hand that brat over like he says. I'm a sheriff."

Mary clutched Avril close, the cane's curved end hooked over her wrist. "The baby is best off in my custody until any legal matters are decided. Surely a circuit judge comes through."

The wall-eyed man moved toward her, one fast stride.

His companion pushed his hat against the fellow's chest to stop him.

"Mrs. Mills here," Coltrain said, "knows she has to obey the law. I'm Sheriff Carpenter's deputy. I gotta take that baby, ma'am, and I will."

"Mrs. Mills" knew there now was a loaded shotgun behind the tall-case clock. She'd never shot one but if she couldn't manage it, she could use it as a club. Along with her cane. Meantime . . . she had to seem cowed, not an easy role.

"Please," she pleaded, backing away. "I've taken care of her for so long." She inched along the wall, a weak woman clinging to a baby and a cane, with no recourse but cringing. A woman postponing the inevitable.

"Now, Mrs. Mills," he coaxed, following her, "you know you gotta do the right thing. Jest give me the baby."

She was almost at the clock. Its ticking sounded as loud as her heartbeat. Such a fine piece of furniture, shipped in from St. Louis, was a prize on the prairie. Now it was her salvation. She glanced toward it as if seeking pathetic shelter beside it. She saw the lethal dark length of the shotgun kept behind it.

Spurs jingled at another capturing step.

Mary slung the crook of the cane low around the deputy's leg and jerked with all her might. He went down in a stream of curses. Her right arm reached out for the shotgun, and got it.

The other man was coming toward her, his face a red mask of rage.

If she could have dropped the baby, she could have shot him.

As it was, she swung the stock hard and grazed his jaw.

His forearm knocked the gun from her grasp.

It hit the floor and exploded with sound and fury.

"Jesus!" the sheriff's voice shouted. "It was kept loaded and cocked." His arm slammed into her jaw. Mary screamed as she and the baby went down. She tried to spiral her body into the wall, holding Avril tight in her arms. Her head was exploding in shock and pain. Then a vicious blow savaged her spine.

Her last memory was of a baby's gurgle suddenly cut off.

* * *

"Ma'am?"

It was a man's voice. The common courtesy sounded like a curse word to her ringing ears.

"Ma'am? Please. What happened here?"

A cool cloth was on her head. Her arms were empty.

"No!"

"Hush," the man's voice said. He cradled her in his arms. The very idea of a man touching her now was terrifying. "You have to be clear and strong. What happened here?"

"My baby."

"I know about your baby. I'll get your baby back."

Mary heard a woman crying and crooning in the distance. Pitiful Constance! What must her poor muddled mind think? Oh. Her own mind was muddled and she wanted to just lie here and hurt and croon and cry.

"Ma'am?" the voice said.

She took a deep breath. "The shotgun."

"You must have winged someone. There's blood drops on the floor all the way to the door and down the stairs to the hitching post."

She felt a rush of savage anger. If only she had killed instead of wounded, weak woman that she was.

Mary blinked her eyes open.

A man's face loomed over hers. His expression was grave but patient. He wore a straight-brimmed black hat, like a city man in the West. What could a city man in the West do for her? She needed an army.

"They took my baby!"

"They?"

She took another deep breath, though every bone in her body ached at the effort. "The so-called deputy!"

"Coltrain, right?"

His knowledge eased her panic. She sobbed. "And the sheriff, a milky-eyed man. One eye."

He was silent for a bit too long. "Quint Carpenter. Right?"

"My baby, my beautiful green-eyed baby. I must get her back!"

"First, you stand." He looked up, away from her. "Ma'am," he said. He had beautiful manners, but what would one expect from an angel of the Lord? Though they didn't usually have tanned faces and mustaches.

Constance was blubbering in the aching corridors of her mind.

"Your sister," he said. "She needs you. I'll get her up, and then you can tend her."

Constance needed her, Mary. Always had.

Strong arms levered her upright and restored her cane to her right hand. A woman's arms went around her. Constance, sobbing. "Mary. Mary! Your poor forehead! You've quite a ghastly goose egg, Mary!"

Then other arms lifted her off her feet and carried her to the bedroom. Constance followed, chattering. "Tea. I'll make you some. Just lay her down there. I'll take care of her. Ah, my dear, thank you so much for coming."

As the holding arms melted away, Mary captured one wrist in a grip of steel, with everything left that was in her.

"The baby. My Avril. They said her father was a man named Noah. I want her back with every beat of my heart, but better her true father should have her than those vicious men. They mean to hurt her."

"I'll get her back," the man's voice said with enough steel in his voice to equal her grip. "You're a brave woman. Trust in the Lord." He pried her fingers away.

She tried to believe him, but nothing would salve her torn heart.

* * *

John Howard Malone hated to abuse good horseflesh, especially a high-stepper he'd won in Fort Worth's Hell's Half Acre, but he slapped the rein ends back and forth over Saber's neck for the first time in their history together, heading for Saint Angela. He'd seen Bear Coltrain and Quint conspiring in the Cactus Saloon and had been suspicious enough to follow them the next day, though discreetly behind.

When they'd led him to this remote little house, he'd wondered if his instincts had been wrong. But, no. Quint would never let go of his quest to kill Noah, not even if it endangered an innocent. Saber had responded to his unprecedented prodding with hard long strides that thrilled the ex-cavalry officer in him and devoured the ground. God, but that out-manned woman had put up a valiant fight! She deserved a knight worthy of her motherly instincts. And so did that baby of Noah's. And Noah.

John Howard Malone finally had found a cause worth fighting for as noble as the Great War of Liberation of the slaves. He winced to think of the rough ride that baby was getting in the custody of those two mean bastards. How had Mary Mills ended up with Noah's baby anyway? He'd have to find out when this was over.

* * *

Saber's coal-black coat was lathered with milky foam, but his forelegs were still prancing sideways as Malone slowed him to a trot when they hit Saint Angela. Saber had a lot of desert Arab in him. Malone thought the horse was probably of finer lineage than he himself.

Malone studied the town's dusty main street, clogged with wagon traffic and ripe with horse droppings. If Coltrain and Quint had expected Noah back here, they'd need information on the soldiers' movements. The notion that greedy, vengeful men would steal a baby to forward their murderous purpose curdled his soul. Had he served in the momentous Civil War so that venal cowards could rule the earth?

Malone's conscience pulsed with regret at leaving that valiant woman behind and alone with her mentally disordered sister. Mary Mills would be in hell until she learned the baby's fate. Yet he knew that he was most needed here, for the sake of his friend Noah, and for Noah's only surviving child.

God! That a man could endure such abuse and repeated losses and still stand. Malone had been granted many advantages in a life he'd lived to the fullest and then thrown away because of a marital betrayal. He'd bloodily avenged that misdeed and still felt no satisfaction, no vindication. He'd been on the run ever since, more from himself than the law. Now, more than in any action in the uncivil Civil War, he was ready to die for more than a cause or a comrade, but for a friend and his child, a man who had saved his life in the war.

Now, at last, he could avenge a wrong done to another, and another, and another, all of them innocents to his frame of mind: Noah, Mary Mills, the infant. This might be a lost cause, as the South had found the war to be, to its enduring regret. John Howard Malone would gain nothing from interfering in these ugly events but a bit of his bitter soul back. And he would do it for that. And maybe for a woman whose soul was satin and steel and true.

*   *   *

"What are we going to do with this thing?" Quint asked.

For the first time Bear Coltrain didn't have an answer.

He was mad as piss about being grazed by that shotgun. It wasn't lethal but his whole left side burned like hellfire. That woman was a pistol. She reminded him of his mama, who took no lip from no man. Six inches to the right and he'd be bleeding to death on the rag rugs of that dirt floor.

And then he'd thought. Since the war some of his restless rage had eased. Being mean and angry all the time took a toll on a body. He saw that things weren't never going to be like they were again. Even him. This is what it had come down to, for some land. Stealing a damn baby. Someone had to carry the baby. He couldn't let it be Quint, despite his own bleeding side. Bear had deserted a wife and babies back in Virginia, out of shame. He couldn't earn enough legal money to keep 'em and had gone to stealing.

Ever since then, getting money had become the only thing that made him feel like a man. That and using his big body and fists to hurt other men so the hurt stopped for a while in himself. He remembered holding kids of his own, not that he much cottoned to the practice. But he knew they needed caring. So he had this squirming bundle of fragile life pressed against his bloody chest as the horse raced on. He'd hunted. He'd fought for the hell of pounding other men into the ground. He'd killed. He'd destroyed. There are many things a man can do, and a few things a man doesn't like to do. And then there are the things a man can't do. He hadn't found one until now, when Quint Carpenter's bloodlust had made Bear Coltrain into a bleeding nursemaid!

Jesus Christ on the Cross! What was he? He hungered. Wanted land. What did this have to do with ripping a baby from a loving woman's arms? Noah? Did he care? Black men were free. They'd soon be all over the place. White men in hoods could satisfy their darkest urges, but they weren't going to change the whole United States of America. Quint had always been a tool, Bear thought. And a fool. But he was a deadly fool.

The little nigger baby cooed against his chest, not knowing color from color, man from woman. Just curls and coos and baby innocence, and, God, he'd give a lot to be back there again himself. Sheriff? Quint was breakin' every law and that could get them both into a heap of trouble. Bear knew his greed had got him twisted up with a crazy killer like a dumb green calf all rolled up in barbed wire.

* * *

They came riding in and dismounted, all squeaks of leather and clinks of spurs and bits. Two men and a bundle. The stable was full of horses and kids. Bastrop kids. The couple that ran the place had gone forth and multiplied endlessly.

A snot-nosed pipsqueak of maybe twelve came to take the reins.

"They're pretty winded, Mr. Coltrain," the Bastrop kid said. "You want me to rub 'em down? Hey, you got blood on you."

"Aren't you the smart one. Yeah, rub 'em down. I'll clean up at the lodging house."

The baby blankets the boy had taken for rags pressed to the sheriff's wound began to squirm and cry.

"That there a baby?"

"None of your business, kid," Quint said, coming around to confront the brat, beefy right arm cocked to wallop him.

"Right, Mr. Carpenter. I'm takin' the horses to their stalls right away." Bastrop Brat Whoever scrambled to grab both sets of reins and lead the horses away over the straw-strewn dirt.

The baby made more of those mewling and cachooing noises that Bear remembered.

"Hey, boys! That a baby you got there?"

Damn! Doodad Buck was coming out from the stall area. Everyone in Saint Angela knew Doodad was a little shy of hay in the loft, but he was one stubborn sonovabitch. Bear with his stinging, bleeding side and a baby in one arm didn't need to piss around with Doodad, who could be real persistent, the way some light-brained folks were.

"Yeah, it's a baby. I gotta get it over to the jailhouse now."

"You arrested a baby, Sheriff? What'd it do?"

Quint prodded Bear in the back.

"It's in protective custody," Bear said, leaving Doodad blinking and Quint giving an evil laugh behind his back. "Just . . . get outta my way. I'm in no mood to palaver."

"That baby is bleedin'!" Doodad stepped closer to look. "By gum, that's my baby! Miz Mary Mills lets me mind it when she's in town. What's happened to it?"

"Nothing, you damn fool! I'm the one that's bleeding. Now get outta my way."

"What're you doing with Miz Mary's baby? Where is she? She'd never—"

Quint pushed around Bear to shove Doodad away.

Doodad stood where shoved, his usually amiable face screwed up with thought.

Bear moved to leave. He'd taken only two steps when he heard a sudden shuffle of boots over straw.

"You can't take Miss Mary's baby to jail!" That was Doodad.

Quint answered with a growl. "I'm the sheriff, you dumb fool. He's my deputy. He can do anything. Now outta our way."

Bear turned to the sounds of two big men meeting in a sudden lunge. Doodad's huge hands were around Quint's neck, pressing his windpipe hard. Quint was trying to claw Doodad's hands away, his face turning scarlet with rage and lack of air.

The baby, maybe sensing the hullabaloo, started in on seriously bawling again. Bear felt a rush of hot liquid on his forearm.

Dammit to hell!

He needed to drop the baby, like Mary Mills had needed to, and . . . and it was one of those things a man can't do, all of a sudden. Thinkin' about his own babies, about the war, his mama even. About slugging that little woman. Maybe jest gettin' tired of always bein' mean.

He halfways thought maybe the world would be a lot simpler without Quint Carpenter in it. No one needed slave catchers now.

Then Quint stopped clawing at Doodad Buck's huge hands and Bear was starting to feel relief, like a wolf trap had just lost its grip on his ankle.

A shot rolled out, a dull clap of thunder to burn your ears off, all fire and brimstone.

Doodad and Quint froze like statues, upright, together in a death grip.

Doodad fell to the stable straw, the Red Sea seeping out around his middle.

"Christ!" Bear couldn't believe it.

Quint was holding his throat and panting, sticking his pistol back in his belt. "Self-defense," he croaked. "You saw it, and I'm the law. Even that damn caterwauling baby saw it maybe. Crazy stupid fool. Let's go find that Noah and trade the brat's custody for his. Lotta things can happen on the trail back to Fort Worth."

Bear went. A man with a baby in his arm can't do much of anything about nothing.

* * *

John Howard Malone had always trusted his luck. It had even helped him escape a murder charge. Maybe it was just instinct in disguise, but he knew he needed an ally if he was going up against Quint Carpenter and Bear Coltrain. He wasn't afraid. He was a cavalry officer again, planning a successful sortie.

So he let Saber cool down while he rode through town and thought. Some folks here knew and liked Noah, as he did. One of them might know where he'd gone and when he'd be coming back. Noah. Malone felt his throat close up as he realized Noah would ride back to find a child he thought he'd lost forever. And he would find that child, safe. Malone would see to that with his last breath, if need be. Who? His eyes roved the unsuspecting townsfolk. They paused on Duff McNamara, setting up his camera outside the Cactus Saloon, his cherubic pink cheeks at odds with the big ten-gallon hat on his dark, curly head. An unreasonable part of Malone's brain blamed the young man not for being at Constance's house earlier this morning when Mary needed help. He was a harmless enough sort, obsessed with photographing what he called "the real West." John Howard Malone, once of Ohio, like Mary Mills, laughed softly to himself. Daily life in the West is earnest, daily life in the West is real, Duff McNamara. You just don't know it yet.

He saw Derwood Buck amble out of the general store, stuffing some loose change in his tight denim pants. Good man. Deadly shot with that Whitworth rifle of his. Maybe. Still, Derwood was always acting as his brother's keeper. Malone needed a man like himself. A man who understood duty, who could act as an officer, alone or with others, with conviction. Without hesitation.

And then an erect figure in a blue uniform rode into sight. Lieutenant Thomas Blaine Gibson from Fort Concho outside of town.

Malone had idled away many non-gambling moments in the Cactus Saloon with Gibson, an educated man from Pennsylvania who loved history and philosophy. His parents had been abolitionists, like Mary Mills' father. He'd been stationed at Fort Concho for six months now and had taken an interest in the green-eyed colored man who could read and write and had survived more danger than the Civil and Indian Wars put together in his own battle for freedom. Gibson despised slavery almost as much as he despised ex-slave catcher and Sheriff Quint Carpenter.

Perfect. Malone nudged Saber over to Gibson's steady bay mount. Military horses knew when to stand and deliver. So did military men, even ex-military men.

"Mornin,'" Malone said, tipping his gambler's hat. He wore his ace-high flush face. "We've got a situation here, involving that Private Freeman of yours."

"I know about it," Gibson said crisply. "I sent Noah off to Fort Stockton just to keep him out of harm's way."

Malone nodded slowly. He knew how to manipulate men to the best advantage in the field of battle and at the poker table. Easy. One step at time.

"I'm purely happy to hear that, Tom. Noah's a good friend of mine from war times. But the sheriff and his associate, Bear Coltrain, took that green-eyed colored baby from Mrs. Mary Mills by force this morning."

"The devil you say! I knew they'd hear about Noah's green-eyed baby being with that Mills woman. The whole town's buzzing about that, gossip bein' the local occupation. Why wasn't the baby with the Bastrops for safe-keeping?" Gibson's right hand went to his pistol. "Mary's all right? My God, that's Noah's baby, though he doesn't know it yet, the only one that survived when Coltrain and Carpenter, God damn their eyes, burned the whole family down in Noah's little cabin. I've been aching for a reason to bring them to account, or just plain put them out of their misery and everyone else's. Is Mary Mills all right? That woman's a saint."

"They hit her with a gun butt, I believe, but she spattered one with a shotgun first. So she's a saint with a stinger." Malone allowed a smile to flit over his grim lips. "She'll be all right, in time. I left her in her sister's care."

"Constance? She's crazy."

"Being needed might fix that a little. The women are all right. It's that baby they took we need to worry about."

"Good God Almighty." Gibson stood in his stirrups to survey the street.

Everything looked normal, buckboards and wagons pulled up to the general store and the feed store. Women strolling on the board sidewalks in front of the shops. Men ambling across the dusty street toward the livery stable or the saloon. . . .

The livery stable.

A roar burst from it, and then Derwood Buck, running hard, came screaming for Doc Tibbs. He paused only to stop at his horse, tied up in front of the general store, and snatch the rifle from the saddle.

Doc Tibbs came out onto his front porch, still sober for the day.

"It's Doodad!" Derwood shouted. "Shot at the livery stable. Come quick!!"

The old man dashed back inside for his ominous black bag and came rushing out.

Malone and Gibson exchanged glances.

"Livery stable," Gibson said.

"They'll need to hole up," said Malone.

"Jailhouse?"

Gibson and Malone gazed at the small frontage. It was bland. Empty. A trap with no exit.

Then a crowd of men came running out of the Cactus Saloon as if pursued by the devil himself.

They nodded at each other and eased their horses toward the saloon.

The animals moved in tandem, not spurred, feeling nothing but their riders' joint purpose. They were military horses. A hullabaloo still erupted from the livery stable. The women in their checked sunbonnets were ducking off the boardwalks into the general store.

Malone and Gibson advanced on the Cactus Saloon.

Only one other person was stirring on that Main Street turned an alley of death.

A big dusty dun horse was walking back into town, mounted by a big dusty colored man with sea-green eyes wearing the uniform of a soldier. Malone reckoned that Noah's ride was coming to its fated end on a good horse with a couple of good friends on his side. What more could a man want in these parts?

The town of Saint Angela had become so quiet you could hear a hat-pin drop.

Maybe Duff McNamara was going to get his saloon shootout photographs, after all.

From the emptied Cactus Saloon, a baby squalled.

Chapter Twelve

by Jeff Guinn

When Acting Sergeant Noah Freeman arrived at Fort Concho leading the bedraggled survivors of the Comanche firefight, he could tell something was wrong. The soldier on guard duty was on edge; he had his rifle on full cock. He kept looking away toward the town like he was expecting someone to come roaring out of it in full attack mode. Noah and his party were waved through, and Noah asked the guard to send somebody for Doc Tibbs. The wounded cavalrymen needed medical help, and there was no army physician assigned to the fort.

"No way Doc's coming out here," the guard said. "He's in town waiting for the gunfight."

"What gunfight's that?" Noah asked.

"Some shooters from Fort Worth are holed up in the Cactus Saloon," the soldier explained. "They gut-shot Doodad Buck, and I'm told he's dying slow. There's lots of guns ready to blast those shooters, but they're safe for now in the saloon because they got some baby as hostage. It's a standoff, but those never last. So Doc's there for when the fighting starts."

The mention of the baby meant less to Noah than the description of the shooters as "from Fort Worth." He knew right away it had to be Quint and Coltrain. Their murderous natures hadn't let them wait until they could turn their guns on Noah.

"This ends now," Noah muttered. "One way or another, it ends."

"What say?" the guard asked, but he was talking to Noah's back. Noah hollered out for the wounded to be taken to the dispensary—he was that comfortable now in his role as acting sergeant—and then he jumped on his horse and pounded along the half-mile or so between the fort and the town.

There was a small group hunkered on the porch of the general store across the dirt street from the Cactus Saloon, and, spread out a little farther away, spectators, mostly men but some women too, people attracted as some always were to the prospect of violence. No one was visible behind the saloon's swinging doors, but there was still the ominous sense of somebody really bad inside there.

Noah pulled up his horse a few dozen yards away from the general store, tethering it to a hitching post and easing his way up to the people there. He picked out Lieutenant Gibson right away, and Doc Tibbs, but most of the others were strangers. Except…

"Captain Malone?" Noah said, sounding as amazed as he felt. "That you, sir?"

Malone turned. "None other, old friend," he replied, and came off the porch for a handshake. Noah couldn't help noticing how strained the captain looked.

"Why are you in Saint Angela, Captain?" Noah asked. "It's a far ride for somebody from up North."

Malone took Noah's arm and pulled him behind the corner of the general store, a smart precaution when armed, desperate men were in a saloon just twenty yards or so away.

"I'm here because some really bad men have come to kill you, Noah," he said. "I wanted to warn you, give you a chance to get away from them."

"I think I already know, Captain," Noah said. "Quint Carpenter for one, with his crazy eye. Bear Coltrain from our old outfit. Well, all right. I got my pistol. I'll go call 'em out and we'll finish this once and for all. I've run as long as I care to."

"It's not that simple, Noah," the captain said. "Wait right here."

Malone eased back to the general store's porch and returned a moment later with Lieutenant Gibson and two men and a woman. Noah knew one of the men. Derwood Buck was acquainted with everyone around Saint Angela, even black soldiers. Noah noticed Derwood's knuckles were extra pale from squeezing the barrel of his fancy rifle so hard.

"They shot my baby brother," Derwood hissed, not so much telling Noah the news as expelling rage too powerful to keep completely bottled up. "I promised Mama I'd watch out for her baby, and I failed her."

"Doodad's not dead yet," Lieutenant Gibson reminded him. "If we can get this standoff concluded, maybe Doc Tibbs can still save your brother."

"They need Doc at the fort, too," Noah interjected. "Lieutenant, I'm back in town 'cause I had to bring in some cavalry survivors of a Comanche fight. Now, this fella's brother might die, and some of those soldiers, if Doc Tibbs can't get to 'em right away. I know who's in that saloon. I've run from 'em for too long. Let's get this over."

Noah reached down to loosen the pistol in his holster, and as he did the thin wail of a baby could be heard from the saloon.

Lieutenant Gibson put his hand over Noah's. "This is more complicated than you realize, Noah. You hear that baby?"

Noah nodded.

"More important, do you know who that baby is?"

"No idea, Lieutenant," Noah answered, trying not to sound as impatient—and insubordinate—as he felt. "Don't matter, anyway. Quint and Coltrain just used it to keep you off 'em 'til they got their chance at me. I'll call 'em out, promise we'll do our shooting and whoever lives afterward rides away clean, and they'll leave that baby right in that saloon. When the shooting's over, you just go in and get it."

"That baby's your daughter, Noah," Gibson said.

Noah felt like he'd been punched hard in the heart.

"My baby daughter's dead, Lieutenant," he said. "Quint and his bunch took her off to kill the night they murdered the rest of my family."

"How many little black baby girls have green eyes like yours, Mr. Freeman?" asked the woman Noah didn't know. She had an ugly lump on her forehead. Somebody had hit her hard, and not long before.

And there, behind the general store, Mary Mills briefly told Noah the story: How she and Duff McNamara found the child on their way from Fort Worth to Saint Angela, how baby Avril Hope—"No, Lovie," Noah automatically corrected—had been hidden for a while from Quint and Coltrain, but finally found and snatched by them.

"I did my best to stop them, Mr. Freeman," Mary added. "But they were quicker than me. I would have died to save your daughter."

"She came close," the man named Duff McNamara said. "And one of 'em, Coltrain or Quint, got hit when Mary's shotgun went off. There was considerable blood on the floor of the house, and not hers."

"Lovie's—?" Noah gasped in horror.

"We're sure it wasn't," Lieutenant Gibson said. "Shotgun blasts are mean things, and if a baby was hit, why, it couldn't survive long. For a couple days we've been hearing loud, healthy cries from inside that saloon, Noah. Once Quint even let a woman bring in a bucket of cow's milk so the baby could eat. They're keeping her fed."

"They're keeping her to trade," Captain Malone said sternly. "You wait. They learn Noah's here, they'll offer a swap. Him for the child. Which, of course, we can't do."

"Why not?" Noah asked. "It's my life, and my baby's."

"Two reasons, Noah," Malone said. "First, these are liars and killers. They're likely to shoot you dead and your daughter, too. Their promise to let the baby go wouldn't mean a thing. Second, from what I've heard and seen they've lived for years killing and thieving without penalty. Why, Quint's a sheriff back Fort Worth way. We can't let them get away with anything else, Noah. Would you want it on your conscience if after this they killed someone else or stole somebody else's child?"

Noah thought hard.

"We just won't let you do it, Noah," Lieutenant Gibson said. "Do I have to have you tied up and taken back to the fort? Now, give me your promise you'll do the best thing and help us wait them out, help us think of a way to finish this without more killing, and you can stay."

Noah didn't reply. He was still stunned to learn his baby girl was alive.

"Noah?" Gibson asked.

"All right," Noah said. Everyone looked relieved but Malone, who knew Noah too well.

He's giving in too easily, Malone thought. We need to watch him close.

By nightfall, Quint and Coltrain knew Noah Freeman was back in San Angela. They found out when they let another woman bring in milk for the baby, and as she set the bucket on the bar she blabbered all about how the green-eyed soldier had come back to town, and now he's acting important-as-you-please sitting with all the white people on the porch of the general store. Ask her, the woman said, she'd rather be scalped by Indians than have to share a porch with niggers, but what could you do? World's a mess. And say, misters, you really aren't going to harm the pickaninny child? Black or not, there was no call to harm a baby.

"We won't unless anybody tries to storm in here," Quint growled. "First thing like that, the baby dies. Tell 'em. Make sure they understand."

Quint allowed only one small lantern to dimly illuminate the back of the saloon, the better to keep shadows from presenting targets to the men across the street. Coltrain, bloody cloths wrapped around his midsection to staunch the bleeding from the shotgun wound to his side, dipped a rag in the bucket of milk. He picked up the baby from the pile of blankets they'd laid her on and began to drip milk into her mouth. Lovie had spent some of the last hours crying with hunger; she eagerly sucked in every drop.

"Last meal we feed that nigger whelp," Quint said casually. "Come sunup, we'll trade her out for her daddy, get this done, get back home."

Coltrain's side burned like hellfire.

"They ain't going to go for it," he said. "This time you went too far, Quint. Some nigger-hunting here and there gets by, but back at the livery you shot a white man, probably killed him. They'll want to hang us for that."

"It was self-defense," Quint said comfortably. Coltrain might be feeling nervous, but not him. He'd taken down a bottle of the best from the shelf above the bar and had some short pulls on it, not enough to get drunk but sufficient to provide that happy whiskey slick. "All we got to do is get out of here in one piece, then get home. Our court ain't gonna do anything to us. We got the circuit judge bought and paid for. In the morning, we make our trade, tie the nigger on a horse, and tell 'em they got to let us go, not follow or anything. If they do, he dies."

Coltrain finished feeding Lovie, who burped and went to sleep. Painfully, Coltrain returned the child to her nest of blankets and dropped heavily into a chair beside Quint.

"You mean we're taking the nigger back with us?" he asked. "Where's the sense there? You going to put him on trial? For what?"

Quint had another small snort. The whiskey burned down his throat. He offered the bottle to Coltrain, who shook his head.

"You don't understand me," Quint said. "We tell them we're trading the pickaninny for her daddy, that we're taking the nigger back with us to put on trial for, shit, we'll think of something. Assault, maybe. He did hit back that time before my boys cold-cocked him. Doesn't matter. It's just the excuse to get our hands on him and go."

"Then what?"

Quint idly spun the chambers of his revolver.

"You know what. Someplace between Saint Angela and back home, that nigger finally will learn there's no escaping Quint. A year, five years, whatever. I set out to catch him long ago, and no nigger's gonna get away from me. He pays for my lost time with his blood."

"And after that?" Coltrain asked, wincing at the pain from his side. There were shotgun pellets buried in there. He hoped the infection wouldn't take until he got home, but he feared it was already too late. There were funny sensations running up and down his arms and legs, and he felt warm from oncoming fever.

"After that, another nigger, and another and another," Quint hissed, sounding just as crazy as he could. "I do love killing niggers so."

Across the way, they took turns standing watch, two at a time. Doc Tibbs had gone off to tend to Doodad—he reported to Derwood that chances were even whether his brother would make it—and then on to the fort and the wounded cavalrymen there. Derwood spent the night at his brother's side, but only after promising he'd keep his rifle handy and be back at the first sign of trouble.

So Captain Malone and Duff McNamara took watch for the first four hours, Noah and Lieutenant Gibson the next four. Malone wanted to team with Noah, but Noah said he and the lieutenant had things to talk over together.

It was shortly before dawn when Noah said softly, "Lieutenant, sir?" The two men were perched on opposite front corners of the general store porch, watching to see if Quint and Coltrain tried to make a run for it. That would be hard for them to pull off successfully. There was no back door to the saloon. Their horses were still stabled at the livery. They couldn't survive the rugged West Texas country on foot. No, when they came they'd have to come through the swinging doors, and that made it easy to watch for them.

"What is it, Noah?" Gibson replied, pitching his voice low, too. Malone, McNamara, and Mary Mills were sleeping on the floor inside. There was no sense waking them until full morning.

"Lieutenant, I want to thank you. You're the only person I ever told my whole story to. You tried to send me away to save me from Quint and Coltrain. Most of all, you showed me respect as a man. God bless you, Captain."

Gibson was deeply moved.

"You're as good a man as anyone who walks, Noah Freeman," he said. "Somehow we're going to find a way out of this. You'll hold your daughter again. God knows his business. Put your faith in him. Look over there —the sun is just rising. The sky is purple and blue and pink all at the same time. A God who can do that kind of natural artwork can save a baby, too."

Noah glanced toward the horizon, just to confirm first light. He eased a little across the porch toward where Lieutenant Gibson sat.

"It surely is a sight," he agreed. "Look out toward that sunrise, Lieutenant. Doesn't it seem to you like there's a flock of birds right in the middle of it?"

"Birds?" Gibson said, leaning forward and squinting hard. "Where do you see—"

Just then Noah hit the lieutenant across the back of the head with the butt of his pistol, hard enough to stun but not cause any permanent damage. Gibson slumped on the porch. Noah checked to see his revolver was loaded and loose in its holster.

"I'm sorry, Lieutenant, but this is the only way," he whispered. "I can't risk my baby dying."

Taking a deep breath, Noah stood up and walked into the dusty street just as the sun rose high enough for the beginnings of thready morning light.

"Quint and Coltrain," he shouted. "You want me? Here I am."

They heard him in the saloon. Quint hadn't been asleep at all. He'd spent the long night hours gently rubbing his pistol between his fingers, thinking of the blood his bullets would soon shed. Coltrain had dozed fitfully, and as Noah's shout woke him up he realized he had the fever good and solid, the infection was all through his body now.

"Fetch the pickaninny," Quint ordered. "Make sure your guns are loaded. We're about to have some action here."

Behind Noah on the porch of the general store, Lieutenant Gibson twitched and moaned. Malone, McNamara and Mary Mills rushed outside.

"What in the hell—" McNamara blurted as he saw Gibson's prone form. Malone called out "Get back over here," to Noah, who was halfway across the way to the saloon, stopping well short of the rickety board sidewalk in front of it.

"No, we're in this now, Captain," Noah yelled back, not taking his eyes off the saloon's swinging doors or his right hand away from the butt of his gun. Malone took a step down from the porch, thinking to maybe grab Noah by the arm and drag him back, but right then the doors swung open and Quint stepped out.

"Finally," he said. "It's over for you, nigger." Quint's had his gun out already; it pointed right at Noah's heart.

"Shoot him and die, Quint," Malone cried. "I'll blow you down where you stand."

"No you won't, mister," Quint replied, talking to Malone but never taking his eyes off Noah. "My partner's got the nigger baby in his arms, and he's pointing his gun at her head. Shoot me, and she's buzzard meat."

"Me for my baby," Noah said, his voice tight. "That's what you want to do. Hand her over, and I'm yours." It was hard for Noah to keep from falling over from all the strain. He wanted his baby to live. He expected he would be dying any moment. And he hated Quint so much.

"The nigger's got it right," Quint said. "Of course, there's conditions. All of you, including Soldier Blue over there"—he gestured to where Lieutenant Gibson was just struggling to his feet—"got to let me and my pard and the nigger ride out free. No following. We see any riders trailing us and we kill him."

"You're going to kill him anyway," Malone said.

Quint grunted out what he probably thought was a laugh, but to everyone else it sounded like a snarl.

"Why, mister, I'm the law back home around Fort Worth," he said. "I been chasing this nigger for assaulting some of my deputies a while back. I plan to bring his black ass into court and let him answer there for his crimes. I don't plan to kill him in front of you unless you leave me no choice."

"Where's my baby?" Noah demanded.

"Everybody stay cool, now," Quint commanded. "Bear, bring her out."

Bear Coltrain was a sorry sight as he staggered through the swinging doors into the street. His face was red and sweaty from fever. Tremors wracked his body. He held, precariously, a small squirming bundle.

Noah automatically reached out to claim his child, and Quint's gun swung back on him.

"Freeze, nigger," he said. "That baby stays with me and my pard for a bit. Now, somebody fetch us our horses from the livery, and one for my prisoner. I want those horses well fed, watered and saddled. Do it now and do it quick."

During the minutes it took for someone to return leading the horses, Quint told Noah to unbuckle his gun belt and let it drop to the ground. Noah did, knowing that giving up his weapon meant giving up his last chance at life. Even if the Captain organized some miraculous rescue attempt, Quint would kill Noah before anyone could stop him.

When the horses were fetched, Quint kept his gun and eyes on Noah while he said, "Bear, get up on your horse and don't let loose of the baby yet." Coltrain barely managed to climb up in the saddle; he came close to dropping Lovie, and Mary Mills uttered a sharp cry.

"Now get on your horse, nigger," Quint told Noah. "No tricks. My pard's just itching to blow your baby's brains out."

Noah shook his head. "I don't mount my horse until my baby's safe," he said. "Give her over to the white lady. Then I'll do what you want."

Quint thought it over. It didn't take him long. "When the nigger's up on his horse, the lady can come take the baby," he said. "Not until. And after, if you want the nigger to live to go to trial, you'll all stay back and not follow. If you do, he dies on the spot, and you'll have had all this trouble for nothing."

"I'll see you get the best lawyer in Fort Worth, Mr. Freeman," Mary called out.

"I'll 'preciate it," Noah replied, knowing it would make no difference. He wasn't going to make it back to Fort Worth alive.

Noah swung up on his saddle. Quint twitched his gun in McNamara's direction.

"Get a piece of rope and bind the nigger's hands behind him," he ordered. Malone might have been tricky enough to pretend to tie Noah, leaving his hands loose enough for an escape attempt. But McNamara didn't know any better than to make the knots tight.

Mary Mills walked briskly over to where Bear Coltrain was mounted and reached up for Lovie. The sick man handed her down, and Mary anxiously pushed aside the blanket the baby was wrapped in.

"She's all right," Mary said and turned back toward the porch of the general store.

"Let me see my baby one last time," Noah said. "I'm begging you, Quint."

While everyone's attention had been on Coltrain, Mary, and Lovie, Quint had quickly jumped into the saddle. Now he was mounted, with his gun still trained on Noah.

"We got no time, nigger," Quint said, exulting in his power over the black man he hated so much. "Time to ride."

But Mary rushed to the side of Noah's horse, holding up the baby. Lovie, jarred by all the sudden motion, cried and waved her little arms. Quint leaned over and yanked the reins of Noah's mount before the former slave could get a good look at his child, but at least he got a fleeting glimpse. He felt an instant sense of peace. His death would be worth it.

"Don't follow us or he dies," Quint reminded Malone and the others. "Let's ride, Bear."

But Coltrain shook his head.

"I'm too weak," he muttered. "I can't go on."

Without hesitation, Quint raised his colt and shot Coltrain through the heart. Before the stunned onlookers could react, he swung the gun back on Noah. "I'll not suffer stragglers any more than I will pursuers," he snarled. "If I'll kill my own pard like that, you better believe I'll shoot the nigger."

His hands bound, Noah twisted in his saddle for one more look at Lovie. Then Quint dug his spurs deep into his mount's side, still hanging on to Noah's reins. They galloped down the street, heading north and east out of town.

Malone's fingers itched to grab his gun, but it was already too late. Pistol range was a few dozen yards. Already, Quint and Noah were beyond that distance.

Mary Mills cuddled Lovie. McNamara led a groaning Lieutenant Gibson to Malone's side.

"What's to be done?" the lieutenant mumbled. "Can someone follow them out of sight?"

"No chance," Malone said, and it was true. All the land around Saint Angela to the north was flat for a half-dozen miles. Quint would spot trackers in a second. And so Malone and the others watched helplessly as Quint and Noah moved 200, 300, 500 yards away.

Another 100 yards, and Quint pulled up, hauling on the reins of Noah's horse so it halted, too.

"What's his game?" Gibson wondered aloud, and Malone shuddered. He knew.

"Quint can't wait to do his killing," he said. "He's out of rifle range and too far to reach in time."

Which Quint knew. Grinning widely, yellowed teeth bared and even his milky eye seeming to glow with malign satisfaction, he sneered, "Off the horse, nigger," and twisted Noah by the shoulder until his captive pitched down into the dust. Since Noah's hands were tied behind him, he couldn't break his fall. He groaned as his shoulder hit the heat-hardened ground.

"Won't hurt long," Quint promised. He jumped off his horse, looking back toward town and satisfying himself that no one in the street could get there to stop what was coming next.

Quint pulled Noah to his knees, drew his gun, stood behind Noah and pressed the pistol to the back of his head.

"For the crime of escaping me," he hissed. "For not knowing your place. For being a nigger!" He pulled back the hammer. "Say your last words."

"Go to hell," Noah spat.

"Die, nigger," Quint said, and there was the crack of the shot and blood and brain tissue in the air.

Noah sagged as Quint's body collapsed on him.

Six hundred yards away, back in the Saint Angela street, Derwood Buck lowered his Whitworth sharp-shooting rifle.

"He shot my baby brother," Derwood whispered. "Now, I shot him."

Epilogue: San Angelo, 1900

"Did it really happen that way, Grandpappy?" the ten-year-old girl
wanted to know.

"All just like I've told you," replied Noah Freeman, about to turn sixty
and long since retired from the army. Now Noah earned his living cleaning and repairing tack for the Fort Concho garrison. He lived with his
daughter Lovie, her husband Jackson, a blacksmith, and granddaughter
Nelly, named for the grandmother she'd never have the chance to know.
Noah doted on the child, but until now he'd never answered her persistent
questions about how he'd originally come to San Angelo—the more mod-
ern name for Saint Angela—and why he'd joined the army in the first
place.

But Lovie had finally said, "Daddy, the girl is ten and old enough to
hear it all. You tell her or I will," and so Noah sat Nelly down and began
talking. The storytelling stretched over several hours, and when Noah
finally got to the part where Derwood Buck's brilliant marksmanship
saved Noah's life and ended the twisted existence of Quint Carpenter,
Nelly's eyes were wide with wonder and fright.

"What if that Derwood man had missed, Grandpappy?" she asked.

Noah smiled. "Well, I expect someone else would have told you this
story. But as you see, it had a happy ending."

"For everybody, Grandpappy?" Nelly wanted to know. "What about all
those others?"

Noah leaned back and reflected. "Derwood Buck, the man who saved
me, had a happy ending, too. His brother Doodad — "

"Funny name," Nelly snickered.

"His brother Doodad pulled through just fine. He survived his gun-
shot and ever after was a special grownup friend to your mama. The Buck
boys moved out to Abilene some years ago, to run their own livery stable.
Sometime if you like I'll take you over in the buckboard to meet them.

"Now, your mama grew up fine and strong. She learned to read and
write from some of the women at the fort, and she met and married your
daddy, who I know is a fine man. Miz Mary Mills really wanted to get out
of Texas after all the shooting and commotion, so she and Duff

McNamara took that crazy sister of hers back to Cincinnati. But 'fore they left, Mr. Duff got those western photos he wanted, pictures of Quint Carpenter lying dead and Derwood Buck posing with his Whitworth rifle. I believe *Harper's* magazine paid a considerable sum for them, and Mr. Duff acquired quite a reputation as a famous photographer."

"And that lieutenant you hit, Grandpappy? Did he live happy afterward?"

Noah sadly shook his head. "There were still all the Indians to fight, and Lieutenant Gibson being a brave man led the troops out after them," he said. "One time, he didn't come back. But before then I'd apologized for smacking him with my pistol, and he understood why I did it. Not all fine men live long lives, I'm afraid. Instead, they make up in good deeds what they lack in time."

Nelly thought that one over for a moment.

"And Captain Malone?" she wondered.

Noah shook his head. "I can't tell you, child. A day or so after all the shooting, he got on his horse and rode off. He was a man who had to keep on the move. He never said, but I assume there was some kind of heartbreak back home that set him on a wandering way. Well, I once saved his life, and he came back and helped save mine, so we're even. God bless him wherever he is."

The little girl stood up and stretched. "So what happens next, Grandpappy?"

Noah was puzzled. "What do you mean?"

Nelly grimaced with the unfeigned frustration all children exhibit when grownups are slow to understand. "So what happens next in this story, Grandpappy? We've come up to right this minute, but where from here? What's going to happen to you and me?"

Noah grinned. "I'm not real sure about what happens to me, child. Sixty's not young. I think my adventures are mostly behind me. But for you, it's different." He gathered Nelly in his arms. "Before you're done, you'll see and do things I could never dream about. See, the more I think about it, the more I think everybody's life is a ride. Sometimes it's easy going and sometimes it's tough. You lose your way and have to find it again. No telling how long the ride's going to last. But you're going to ride fine and far, and someday you'll tell your children, even your grandchildren, about old Grandpappy Noah and all that happened to him."

"Live forever and tell them yourself, Grandpappy," Nelly suggested.

"I'll sure give it a try," Noah promised, and the old man and girl hugged, their matching green eyes shining with pleasure at each other's company and the promise of more good times to come.

Editors' Note

Ten years ago, a group of writers met from time to time in the TCU Press office to kick around the idea of a collaborative novel using themes from western fiction. Mostly we talked about Frank James, Jesse's brother who sold men's suits in Dallas but lost his job because people came in to hear his stories but didn't buy the suits.

Jerry Flemmons was a mainstay of that group—was it his original idea? Probably — and when health prevented him from continuing, the project just sort of fell apart. The time wasn't right.

But in the fall of 2005, things got back on track. Jeff won't admit it, but he was the driving force behind reviving the project. And he got the *Fort Worth Star-Telegram* interested. We chose a basic plot line and handed it over to Elmer Kelton to start, as he most capably did. As each author finished a chapter, it was forwarded to the other authors so that all could keep current and prepare themselves for their own chapters. We asked each to contribute 5,000 words in about two weeks. Because they are professionals, they met our deadline.

It was a particular pleasure to work with Mary Dittoe Kelly, our unpublished author who won the *Star-Telegram* online contest for a chance to participate, another of Jeff's good ideas.

Still, assembling a collaborative novel isn't without its harrowing moments. Sometimes new directions for the story surprised us and required minor juggling in earlier chapters; other times, we simply had to tweak the material that came to us to make as smooth a story flow as possible. It was a challenge, but it was also fun. And through it all, we remained friends—no small accomplishment, that!

We don't intend to submit *Noah's Ride* for a Pulitzer, but we do think it's a great showcase of what authors can do in collaboration. And it's a pretty good western novel!

Judy Alter
Jeff Guinn
Fort Worth 2006

Reflections from the Novice

Jeff and Judy asked me to describe my experience being the never-before-published, dreaming-for-all-my-life-of-being-published, still-pinching-myself-to-be-sure-I'm-really-being-published, contest-winning author of Chapter 8 of *Noah's Ride*.

My happiness seems boundless. To create pure fiction, to breathe life into characters that have never before walked the earth, to know that readers will be turning my pages and responding to them one way or another . . . well, that has been the dream of my life!

Crafting my 200-word contest entry was quite a challenge. I invoked the spirits of Roy, Dale, Gene, Clint, and Rowdy, all cowpersons who got right to the point.

Jeff and Judy had specific instructions for me once they'd informed me I had won; they both commanded, "Mary, have fun!" I thank them for that . . . it has been fun every step of the way. Though I felt a tremendous responsibility to honor the characters who were delivered to me in chapters 1-7, I also enjoyed every minute of my writing as I took Noah a bit farther along on his ride.

There were so many good entries! I thank God for letting it be my turn and for giving me parents who taught me that words hold magic.

Mary Dittoe Kelly

About the contributors

Phyllis Allen is a short story writer and essayist who in 2005 won a national competition to have some of her work featured on National Public Radio's *All Things Considered.*

Judy Alter is director of TCU Press, author, and 2005 recipient of the Owen Wister Award for Lifetime Achievement from Western Writers of America, Inc.

Mike Blackman, former executive editor of the *Fort Worth Star-Telegram*, currently holds the Warner Chair at Sam Houston State University where he teaches reporting, feature writing, and editing.

Mike Cochran is a longtime, award-winning reporter for *The Associated Press* and the *Fort Worth Star-Telegram*, whose books include *Texas v. Davis.*

Carole Nelson Douglas, a former newspaper reporter and editor, is the author of fifty novels and has won or been short-listed for more than fifty writing awards. She writes the Midnight Louie feline PI contemporary mystery series set in Las Vegas and the Irene Adler Sherlockian historical suspense novels.

Jeff Guinn is the former *Fort Worth Star-Telegram* book editor and author of ten books, including *Our Land Before We Die*, the nonfiction winner of the 2003 TCU Texas Book Award, and *The Autobiography of Santa Claus*, a national best-selling novel.

Mary Dittoe Kelly is the winner of the *Star-Telegram* "You Be the Author" competition and Religious Education Coordinator at Good Shepherd Catholic Community.

Elmer Kelton is currently America's best-selling author of western American fiction. His works include *The Time It Never Rained* and the Hewey Calloway trilogy: *Two Bits a Day, The Good Old Boys*, and *The Smiling Country*. Mr. Kelton has been recognized for lifetime achievement by Western Writers of America, Inc., the Texas Institute of Letters, and the Western Literature Association.

James Ward Lee is the author of *Texas, My Texas, Adventures With a Texas Humanist*, and co-editor of *Literary Fort Worth.*

James Reasoner is a professional author of over 180 novels, including westerns, crime fiction, private eye novels, and other genres.

Mary Rogers is an award-winning features writer and columnist for the *Fort Worth Star-Telegram.*

Carlton Stowers has twice won the Edgar Award for true crime writing from the Mystery Writers of America. His newest title is *When Dreams Die Hard: A Small Town and Its Six-Man Football Team.*

Jane Roberts Wood is the author of numerous novels, including the classic *Train to Estelline.*